TRY NOT TO DIE

Super High

MARK TULLIUS

STEVE MONTGOMERY

VINCERE
P R E S S

Published by Vincere Press
65 Pine Ave., Ste 806
Long Beach, CA 90802

Try Not to Die: Super High
Copyright © 2025 by Mark Tullius & Steve Montgomery

Printed in the United States of America
First Edition

ISBN: 978-1-961740-40-2
Cover by Jun Ares

I dedicate this book to my mom and dad. My mother, who always encouraged my creativity, often wrote alongside me. My father, with his love of sci-fi and horror films, helped shape my imagination. This story belongs to them both.

Steve

To all the readers who have made questionable decisions—

and lived to tell the tale

Mark

A Note From the Authors

Working on this book with Mark has been an absolute pleasure. He reached out to me at the height of COVID with a title and a vision, and after some incredible discussions, he gave me complete creative freedom to bring this story to life. His guidance has been invaluable, and he's become a true mentor in my writing journey. I hope readers connect with the characters and get completely immersed in the adventure we've created!

Steve

My history with Steve Montgomery goes back nearly 20 years to when we trained together at the Florence Fight Farm in South Carolina. At the time, Steve was a teenager, and I only lived in the state briefly, so we didn't get to know each other well. Years later, we reconnected when I traveled to American Top Team in Florida to interview him and his teammates for *Unlocking the Cage: Exploring the Motivations of Mixed Martial Artists*. I already had a ton of respect for Steve before that trip, but seeing firsthand the kind of friend, fighter, and person he was only deepened my admiration. During that visit, I also discovered his passion for writing, and it was just a matter of time before we found the perfect project to collaborate on.

Due to our busy lives, this book had its share of stops and starts, but we pushed through—something martial arts had trained us to do. One of the most rewarding parts of this journey was the opportunity to learn and grow together. Just as Steve sharpened my jiu-jitsu and striking skills, I was able to share writing techniques, watching him develop and refine his craft with each meeting. On our final 2.5-hour call to finalize the book, I was blown away by his creative decisions and how much he was improving my sentences. Just as my goal in martial arts was to hold my own against my instructors, Steve proved himself my equal as a writer.

I couldn't be prouder of this book or more excited to collaborate on a second *Try Not to Die* with Steve.

Mark

TRY NOT TO DIE: SUPER HIGH

Florida skies must be one of the most beautiful displays anywhere in the world. The pink clouds scattered like paint across a light blue backdrop, the fading sun illuminating all the reds, oranges, and purples... But regardless how spectacular a Miami sunset may be, I'm still focused like a hawk.

I've always paid close attention to particulars, sometimes to my own detriment. It's probably why I love competitive shooting so much. The endless details involved in the sport are the drug that keeps me high.

Being here is surreal. It's my first year competing as a professional, and I'm one run away from winning the Sig Sauer 3-Gun National Championship. After all the sacrifice and hard work, I made it—barely an adult and beating people way more experienced.

The PA system buzzes. "Up next, the Tactical Division finals. Calling Jake Swisher and Scott Blevins to stage number three. You two are on deck. Once again, in the Tactical Division finals, calling Jake Swisher... and Scott Blevins, to stage number three."

My heart's beating hard enough to bruise a rib, but my breathing technique slows it down. The closer I get to the stage, the warmer my blood gets. I set my range bags on the table to the left and unpack.

Strutting my way is the five-foot-two Scott Blevins. He's wearing a smug grin with his chest puffed out. Blevins was Dad's rival for years, and I've never seen a side of him to like.

Instead of using the open table to the right, Blevins sets his bags next to mine. "Jake Swisher," he says in his screechy little voice. "Didn't plan on embarrassing *you* today."

I don't even look over. For the past six months, I've been dealing with his trash talk. Blevins wins if I give him one drop of emotion, so I rack the slide of my custom Zevtech Glock, gliding it like butter along the rails.

Blevins chuckles and unzips his rifle bag, taking his sweet time. "Truth is, I never thought you'd make it past the first round."

Today's gone too well for me to lose focus now. Winning the $50,000 prize money would be incredible, but there's also more sponsors scouting for new talent here than at any other event. I keep my lips shut and slip the last few shotgun shells into my belt, next to the pistol magazines. Every meticulous detail must be perfect. A quarter of a second could be the difference between fame and failure.

Blevins is inches away. The stench of halitosis and tobacco is overwhelming. "You actually think you can hang with the pros, huh?" he says, glaring up at me.

His hair's receded far enough to blend with the bald spot on his oversized dome, but I keep quiet.

"You're just gonna look at me like some moron?" he says. "I get it. Too scared to talk."

In all their time competing, Dad never let Blevins get to him. So, I put on my biggest grin and say, "Yep, that must be it."

Dad's twin brother, Shawn, is heading our way through the crowd like a 250-pound, bearded bowling ball in a red flannel shirt. Military tattoos cover the meaty forearms exposed by his rolled-up sleeves.

"Everything all right here, gentlemen?" Uncle Shawn asks through a fake smile. "I know we're not gonna have any unsportsmanlike conduct on *my* range today, are we?"

Blevins laughs. "Me? Unsportsmanlike?"

The meaty wrinkles across Uncle Shawn's forehead tell me he's low on patience for Blevins. "I was talking to both of you." Shawn built the Everglades Shooting Center from nothing and has been running it for twenty years. He has no problem reminding us he's the boss.

I smile and say, "I'm just here to win."

Blevins' cheeks go red. "You Swishers are all the same... Snowflakes. Don't get butthurt 'cause I'm 'bout to smoke your nephew on your own doorstep." He narrows his eyes at me. "Home field advantage ain't gonna help you today, boy. This ain't the Little Leagues no more. You're banging with the pros now." Blevins snatches his bags and sets them on the other table. "You're banging with Scott 'Lionheart' Blevins."

"Swisher!" a range officer calls. "Jake Swisher! Let's go! Time to make ready!"

Uncle Shawn pats me on the back. "Go get it, Jake. It's your time. Stay dialed in and let your instincts take over, stud."

When Dad died six months ago, I would've been lost without Shawn and his son, Geo, who's over in the stands. "I won't let you down," I tell Shawn. "This is *our* house!"

The range officer takes me on a tour of the course. First up is the rifle portion, fifteen targets placed at distances between ten and two hundred yards away. Then I'll swap for my shotgun and have ten more targets at random distances. Last is the pistol course, a mixture of twenty steel and paper bullseyes to hit while navigating a plywood structure. The limits on magazine capacity will force at least one reload of each gun.

Blevins is waiting for us at the staging area. "This virgin's cherry is 'bout to get popped."

Lionheart might not have any tact, but he does hold the fastest completion time for this stage at one minute and ten seconds. He did it last competition in the finals without missing a single shot. The asshole *can* shoot straight.

My weapons are lined up just right, my pistol magazines positioned in the correct direction. The grip tape on my rifle magazines is perfectly exposed for my fingers to clasp.

"Right here, sir," the range officer says, pointing me to the starting line.

I dig my feet into the dirt and make sure my range glasses and ear plugs are securely in place. The fading sunlight has been replaced with large, overhead floodlights. I take a deep breath. On the exhale, I think of Dad and slow my heart rate.

"Range is hot! Range is hot!" the range officer yells from behind me. "Shooter ready?"

I nod, my eyes locked in on the eighteen-inch steel circles forty-five yards away.

The range officer raises the timer. "Stand by!"

The starting timer blares like a fire alarm. I grab my custom AR rifle from the table and slap the first two plates with 5.56 rounds. Two hundred yards away, two steel gongs ring like church bells. I sprint toward the maze of blue barrels and stalk paper silhouettes, placing two shots into each bullseye. My hand finds a new magazine to reload while I exit the cluster of barrels. The last two steel gongs are seventy-five and eighty-five yards away, on opposite sides of the course. In under three seconds, they're added to my tally. With the safety on, I slide my rifle into a forty-gallon drum and grab my shotgun from the one beside it.

My movements are precise. The rapid fire of the shotgun booms when I blow away all five paper silhouettes. As I sprint, I slide more shells into the magazine tube without missing a beat and dive into a prone position. Two clay silhouettes hang beyond a small window. Both get blown away. I push myself off the floor like it's on fire, raising the red dot sight to meet the last three paper villains. Every round meets its mark.

I discard the shotgun into an empty drum and draw my pistol. The first ten targets are a row of six-inch plates. I aim and pull the trigger before I can even see my red dot. The sound of screaming steel returns after every bang. I drop the magazine and insert a fresh one, then enter the plywood building. After turning right, I fire, sprint left, and fire twice, my core muscles flexing with every twist and turn. The last gong is thirty yards in front of the exit. It takes me less than two seconds to aim and fire. It's still singing as the buzzer sounds.

I finished the course without missing.

"Unload and show clear!" the range officer yells.

I drop the magazine and rack the slide to show my gun is empty. My inhales are slowing down, the adrenaline dump hitting me all at once.

"One minute and five seconds. No penalties," he yells over his radio.

I can't believe I just beat Blevins' record by five seconds. Uncle Shawn and Geo are going crazy in the stands.

"Congrats, kid," the range officer says. "That was a hell of a run. Nice work."

The shooting range staff makes gathering my guns and magazines a breeze.

Before I can even load any gear into my range bags, Uncle Shawn is all over me, his big burley hands clasping my shoulders. "You just broke the record, Jake! I know your dad better than anyone ever did, and I promise you, he's so proud of you!"

Right behind him is Geo, who's always been more of a big brother to me than a cousin. People always say we look like twins, both of us being six foot four with dirty blond hair. "You did it, J-Bone! No way he's gonna beat that time!"

"I already tallied up your scores," Shawn says. "If Blevins doesn't finish the course in a minute fifteen without penalties, you'll win."

"J-Bone! Way to represent on home turf!"

Blevins flanks us from behind. "A minute fifteen'll gimme enough time for Starbucks afterwards." He looks directly at me. "Sorry, baby boy. I wouldn't get your hopes up. Last year's time was on a bad day."

Blevins walks over to the range officer to prepare for his run.

"He's full of shit. He ain't gonna finish under that time," Shawn says, although he sounds a little doubtful.

I'm nervous too. Scott Blevins might be a clown, but the man is a world-class competitor. He's been head-to-head with Dad many times, and my father was twice the shooter I could ever hope to be.

Every piece of gear I put away reminds me of Dad. Even when he was alive, I constantly missed him. He was always out of the country, doing some kind of work for the military. Most of the time, he couldn't even tell me where he was going. Since he died down here last winter, I've been trying to come to terms with the fact I'll never truly know my father.

Training and competing full-time hasn't helped me get over him. Every time I'm at the range, I think about the day Uncle Shawn called me with the news. I'm reminded of the things I never got to say to him. Why can't I be strong like Dad was? He could've gotten over *me* dying. I'll never be as tough as my father. Or Uncle Shawn, for that matter. They're grizzled Navy Seals who spent years serving our country. Filling their shoes seems impossible.

Blevins approaches the starting line and readies himself. The range officer begins the time.

Blevins smokes the first two steel targets with ease, but it takes him three shots to hit both gongs at two hundred yards, which costs him a penalty point. Even through the gunfire, I hear his high-pitched swearing. He's frustrated but making up for his mistake, exiting the maze of blue barrels and nailing the last two targets.

Blevins picks up his shotgun and trips when he starts to run. He snatches the gun off the ground and pulls the trigger by mistake, blowing up a huge chunk of dirt in front of him.

"Negligent discharge," the range officer shouts, his waving arms signaling Blevins' run is over.

Geo wraps his long arms around my neck from behind, choking me while kissing the side of my head. Uncle Shawn walks toward the officials. I can't believe this is real. My first competition on the professional circuit and I just won the Sig Sauer 3-Gun National Championship. Fifty thousand dollars is going to change my life.

Blevins grabs his guns and stalks back, yelling at the range officer. "What the hell, man? Someone moved the shotgun after I positioned it!"

The range officer shakes his head.

"Nobody gave me time to shake dirt out of my magazines in between runs. They just called me over here right away." Blevins slams his hat on the ground. "It's why I missed the first time! I deserve another run, man!"

The range officer ignores him. "Off the course."

Blevins shoves the officer, and they begin tussling. Several other range employees sprint over and break them up, stripping Blevins of his shotgun.

Blevins says something about it being bullshit and stomps my way.

I hate confrontation, but Geo's the opposite of me and loves a good fight, verbal or physical. He steps in front of me and shouts at Blevins. "Nice run, Scott! Definitely faster than last year's! Less than a minute!"

"What the hell'd you say to me, Swisher?"

Geo's barely able to keep a straight face. "Just congratulating you on breaking last year's record."

Blevins turns to me. "You think 'cause you won a tournament on your family's range that somehow you're on my level?"

I've had enough of him. "Dude, I'm over a foot taller than you. How do you think you're on my level?"

Geo bursts into laughter, which only pisses off Blevins even more.

"You ain't nothing but Steve's un-aborted crotch fruit!" Blevins yells. "Your daddy was a fat turd who sunk the second he hit the water. Oughta sink your skinny ass with a cinder block too! We can put ya right next to him, out there in the swamp!"

If my tongue were between my teeth, it'd be split in half. Dad drowned in a fan boat accident, fishing with Uncle Shawn in the Everglades. This rotten-breathed puke of a man is hurling insults at the son of a dead Navy Seal. I should knock him out before Geo steals the chance. But if I start a fight, I'm definitely getting disqualified.

*****

Keep it cool and collect my prize money.
Turn to page 11.

Get in Blevins' face and challenge him to a fight.
Turn to page 47.

The Humvee is headed right for us, and I didn't go through all this just to get crushed. I scramble toward the backyard and tell Alex and Geo, "This way."

Geo runs ahead and stops at the garage. "There's nowhere to go!"

"Gotta jump it," I say, pointing out the small brick wall dividing the properties.

"Neither one of us can climb that," Alex says.

"I'll boost you," Geo says, setting his AK on the top of the wall. "You first," he tells me, "but stay up there until we're over and can lower you down."

I set the Glock next to the AK and pull myself up on three, laying on the edge, my leg screaming at me.

Geo hoists Alex up a little further down. Alex swings his leg over, and it smacks my foot. I scream, tumbling off the other side.

I crash onto hard dirt, my shoulder dislocated. I roll onto my back and gunfire erupts on Geo's side of the wall. Alex grunts and lands a few feet away, no movement.

Geo grabs the AK off the wall and opens fire. I try to stand, but can only get to a knee, my leg bandage completely soaked with blood.

The rat-a-tat-tat of the AK stops, and there's just hooting and hollering on that side of the wall. A deep growl on mine.

I hope it's Alex fighting through pain, but that growl is too deep, too animalistic. Fuck.

I don't know where the dog is, only that he's running right for me about to attack. My gun's the only hope. I throw myself against the wall and reach for the Glock with my good arm.

My hand touches metal, but the dog slams into me and the gun falls. Sharp teeth tear into my hamstring.

"No!" The German Shepard's head whips back and forth, ripping through my muscle. I can't punch it with my right arm, nothing I can do to stop it from its attack.

The dog drags me away from the wall and breaks off from my leg. I flip onto my back and raise my hand for protection, but it lunges on me. My hand is pinned between the dog and my chest, and I can't stop its teeth from sinking into my throat.

***

The correct choice was to wait for the Humvee to pass.
Turn to page 117.

Blevins' face is begging me to bash it, but I take a deep breath and blow it out. "You ain't worth it," I say, turning my back on him. "I've got my money to collect."

"Fuck that," Geo says, his fist flying, connecting with Blevins' jaw and dropping him to the ground. "No one talks shit about my uncle."

Blevins grabs his jaw with his left hand and butt scoots back. "Broke it," he mumbles, his eyes wide with anger.

"Goddamn right I did," Geo says turning to Uncle Shawn who's running towards us with the officials right behind him.

Blevin draws his pistol so fast I barely have time to push Geo out of the way.

Boom!

A hot fire pierces my neck, warm blood spurting out both sides. I try to speak but only more blood comes out.

Uncle Shawn jumps on Blevins and wrestles the gun from him as I fall to my knees, trying to stop the blood flowing from both holes.

"Medic! Medic!" Geo screams. "Help!"

I drop on my ass and tip over, the blood pouring through my fingers, running into my throat. I choke.

Geo sits me up, trying to keep me elevated. "You're alright," he says.

I suck down blood trying to breathe and cough up more. My heart beats so fast, my head feels like it's going to explode.

"You're gonna be alright." Geo says. "Keep your eyes open."

But I can't. Can't open my eyes. Can't hold on.

***

The correct choice was to get in Blevins' face and challenge him to a fight. Turn to page 47.

"That wasn't a methhead," I say. "Stop the truck."

Geo does, but isn't happy about it. "Really, dude?"

"Maybe it's one of those people your dad was talking about."

"You mean, *warning* us about?"

"Since when did you become a little bitch?" I say, knowing full well how to get him to comply.

He reaches across me and pops open the glovebox. "Go ahead, Mr. Eagle Scout, but take that with you. My little bitch ass will be chilling in the AC."

It's dark as hell outside the truck and this is a stupid idea, but I can't back down now. And imagine how proud Uncle Shawn will be if I capture one of these whackos. I take the Glock from the glovebox and check it's loaded even though I doubt Geo would ride with it unreadied.

"You going or can we go have some fun?"

"I'll be right back," I say, opening the door and stepping into the humid night.

"Close it."

"Yeah, yeah," I say, slamming the door a bit harder than I should have. It's too dark to see outside of the truck's brake lights. I take out my phone and put on the flashlight, aim it at the section of the woods the woman disappeared into.

The night is silent except for the low rumble of the Tacoma. I keep to the road and spot drops of blood where the lady grabbed the racoon. I follow the trail to the edge of the trees, no longer able to hear the truck, only soft chirps and sounds of the swamp.

Honk!

I jump so high both feet leave the ground, my heart racing. "You motherfucker!" I shout at Geo who's busting up, looking at me in his rearview.

He rolls down his window and sticks out his hand to wave me forward. "Come on, dude!"

The ground past the trees is muddy and I'm just wasting time, probably a sorry attempt to delay the inevitable social interaction. "Alright, alright," I say, flipping off the light and pocketing my phone. "I'm coming."

Something rustles behind me, slams into my back before I can spin around. I hit the dirt face first, dropping the pistol, pushing to get the snarling woman off me.

"Jake!" Geo shouts, his door opening.

The light from the truck illuminates the woman's blood-splattered face as she lunges for my neck.

I raise my forearm to block her, and she latches on to it with her teeth, tears out a chunk right below my wrist, the most pain I've ever felt.

"The gun!" Geo yells. "Where's the gun?"

I can't answer, too busy trying to use my other hand to keep the woman off me. But she won't stop, her nails raking the flesh from my face, trying to gouge my eyes.

Geo grunts and kicks the woman, but she's not stopping, sinking her teeth into my neck.

"What the fuck!" Geo shouts as the woman whips her head back and forth.

Boom! Boom! Boom!

The woman falls off me but takes the front of my throat with her, a fountain of blood spraying my face.

***

The correct choice was to follow Geo's lead and not worry about it. Turn to page 19.

There's no way our car's making it through the roadblock, and the mob will be all over us if we try to throw it in reverse. "To the right," I tell Geo, pointing at the closest driveway.

Geo punches the gas and whips the wheel, bouncing us up the curb and onto the sidewalk, the mob running toward the car. "Get down!" he yells at us.

I stay seated and ready the Glock, duck when a rock smashes into my window.

Geo swerves left and slams the accelerator to the floor, heading straight for the dozens of people lined up between the roadblock and the yellow one-story house.

A board bounces off the hood. A shovel bangs off the rear passenger door. A flaming torch is tossed on the windshield. The crowd stands its ground.

"Fine," Geo says, gritting his teeth and aiming at the big guy in front, wielding a crowbar.

The anger on their faces turns to surprise when Geo doesn't stop, the bodies flying, several smashing our windshield into a spiderweb of cracks.

We fly past the next house, Geo angling back toward the street. "I can't see—"

Crash! The car slams to a halt, my head whipping forward, a broken brick mailbox blocking us.

Geo locks all our doors. "They're coming!"

Bodies swarm the car, a few jumping on the hood and kicking at the windshield. A branch is thrown through Geo's already-broken window, a shovel clanking off the roof.

Bam! Bam! Bam! Geo drops three of them, my hearing gone. I put two rounds into the assholes on the hood, another two into a guy trying to stab Geo with a knife. All I hear are vibrations and my ears ringing.

The mob falls back, and Geo says, "Bail!" He throws his door open and fires at the closest rioter, dropping him.

I unlock my door and step onto the yard, swiveling to make sure no one sneaks up behind. Alex and Brianne are banging on the passenger window, mouthing, "It's locked!"

"Shit! Cover me." Geo reaches into the car and comes out with the keys.

I train my gun on the closest rioters, who've retreated behind the roadblock.

Geo unlocks the rear door and helps Alex exit the vehicle. The door to the house behind me swings shut, and a woman in a hoodie and bandana charges, a gallon-sized Molotov cocktail in her hands.

I swivel and fire, putting a bullet in her chest, but the jug has already left her hands and is flying for the trunk of the cruiser. The car goes up in flames and blows Geo and Alex several feet back. Brianne, who's still in the car, drops to the floorboard, covering her head and screaming.

Alex rolls on the ground, trying to put out the fire on his left shoulder and arm. Geo flips over to his stomach and fires at the three men charging. He drops the skinny guy holding a knife, but the other two keep coming.

Geo's gun clicks empty.

I put a bullet into each of the men rushing Geo, but the rest of the mob closes, someone shouting that Geo's out of bullets.

Geo gets to his feet and tries to help Alex, but the swarm engulfs them—kicking, punching, swinging boards and branches.

The angry ball of bodies runs into the flaming car, knocking the passenger door closed and locking Brianne in the backseat.

I imagine their heads are metal targets and place five direct hits, barely missing the bearded guy with dreads. The crowd scatters, leaving Geo and Alex curled up on the ground.

Geo takes the shovel from a dead man's hands. Alex is semi-conscious, bleeding from his head and badly burnt on his left shoulder and arm. Geo grabs Alex's collar and drags him toward the house.

I jump on the hood of the cruiser, kicking in the windshield before realizing it won't help Brianne—there are bars between the front and back seat. The flames swell, and I'm afraid we don't have long before they reach the nearly full gas tank.

The keys aren't in the door. They must've fallen to the ground when Geo got attacked. I jump and flip over bodies, one eye on the rioters and the other on the ground. The third body I roll over has been covering the silver keyring.

I'm picking up the keys when the gas tank blows, knocking me on my ass. The entire passenger compartment is in flames, and I'm grateful I can't hear Brianne's screams.

Geo and Alex run into the backyard of the house with the brick mailbox. I chase after them and catch up behind the garage, where Geo's reloading the revolver with shells from his pocket.

Alex is staring at his seared skin, a high-pitched wail coming from his pursed lips.

"Got to keep quiet," Geo says, closing the revolver's cylinder.

I peek around the corner. "They're gonna kill us," I warn him.

"Where's Brianne?" Alex asks through clenched teeth.

I can't tell him.

"They shot her," Geo says.

"What the fuck? I'll kill all you motherfuckers!" Alex screams at the night, pulling away from us.

Geo runs after Alex and grabs him, but there are already people heading our way.

"They're in the backyard!" someone yells from the front. "Over here!"

There's a tall wooden fence at the very back. We run to it and help Alex over before hopping into the next backyard. The gang of masked looters is hot on our trail.

"This way," someone shouts from behind. Gunshots erupt, bullets blowing through the fence we just jumped over.

"Keep going," I say, pointing toward the side fence, which is shorter than the last one.

Alex goes first, but the fence is wobbly, and he falls to the ground, landing on his burnt shoulder and screaming in pain.

Two rioters jump the back fence, and several more are running down the driveway. There's got to be at least ten of them, and they're going to be on us any second.

*****

Follow Alex and Geo over the fence.
Turn to page 123.

Shoot my last five shots at the looters who are closing in.
Turn to page 86.

Our car's so jacked up there's no way we can crash through that roadblock or jump the curb. "Reverse it," I say as the mob closes in.

Geo puts it in gear and hits the gas, but the engine only roars.

"It's in neutral!" I tell him.

He shifts to P and back to R, hitting the gas with the same result. "Fuck!"

Rocks smash into the shattered windshield, and the mob's rushing us from all sides. "Through them!" I say as a board breaks Geo's window.

He slams it into drive, but we don't move. The transmission is completely gone. "Shoot 'em," he says, undoing his seatbelt and pulling out his revolver.

We're surrounded by more people than we've got bullets, but I put a hole in one of the bastards that just scrambled on the hood.

Brianne's shouts of terror turn to pain, and Alex screams for help. I turn and put a round in each of the guys pulling her out by her hair. But a more immediate problem heads our way: a flaming bottle flying right at us.

The Molotov cocktail smashes into the backseat, the flames engulfing the entire car. Geo stops shooting and opens his door only to have it slammed shut on him, the fuckers on my side doing the same thing.

I fire blind through my window, but I'm being roasted alive, the fire burning my throat....

***

Try again. Turn to page 83.

I'm not convinced what we saw *was* just a homeless person, but I say, "All right, all right. Keep driving."

"Thank you. You were starting to sound like Dad for a second. Your shirt was turning flannel on me."

We continue speeding east toward town. The Saturday night lights of South Florida emerge on the horizon. Geo gives me the low-down on everyone I'll be meeting. The person whose house we're going to, Alex Paulsen, is one of Geo's best friends from the University of Miami. Apparently, he's renting a dope mansion where he throws all sorts of parties. Geo keeps going on about the girls who will be there, swerving off the road every time he shows me their socials.

After ten minutes of weaving through ritzy Miami suburbs, Geo turns into a fancy driveway. Alex's parents must be filthy rich. The stained-glass window surrounding the front door has to be fifteen feet tall. A group of people are taking shots on the massive porch, and two guys approach our car.

Geo rolls down his window. "What's up with you mutants?"

The taller one in the bright red button-up shirt with fluorescent white stripes steps forward. He ducks his head enough to keep his spiked, black hair from touching the car and leans in the window. "You tell me, ladies? Y'all looking to do some dirty deeds dirt cheap?"

"I'll do some dirty deeds, but it'll cost ya," Geo says. "This is Jake. Jake, this freak in the stop sign shirt is Alex."

"What's up, man?" I lean over and shake his hand through the car window. "Good to meet you. I'm Geo's cousin, unfortunately."

"Sucks for you. I'm gonna guess it's his fault y'all are late." Alex points to the guy beside him. "Oh yeah, this is my boy, Peter, a.k.a. Peter Pan."

The shorter, stockier guy in a blue polo shirt reaches past Alex and shakes my hand. "Peter Stern, good to meet you."

"All right, enough hugs and kisses. Get out and let's go," Alex says. "These ladies just took some molly, so they're getting restless."

"Okay, Okay." Geo unbuckles his seatbelt and gets out. "Maybe next time, give me more than thirty minutes' notice."

I'm pretty sure molly is a form of ecstasy, but I don't ask. If the girls know what a square I am, it might kill my chances with any of them. I follow the guys toward the porch, where the girls are looking at us and giggling. Competitive shooting is one challenge I'm comfortable with, but women are an entirely different ball game.

"You shoulda been here the last couple of hours," Alex says. "We've been getting trashed. The boys have been smoking blunts. The girls have been taking shots, son!"

The closer I get to the porch, the more it smells like Alex is telling the truth.

Geo pushes me right up to the steps for an unwanted introduction. "Hello, lovely ladies. It's great for you all to see me again."

The girls smile and roll their eyes. The beautiful brunette kissing his cheek must be Tiffany.

"I come bearing a wonderful gift," Geo says. "My cousin, Jake, from South Carolina just won the biggest professional shooting competition in the country today. He's a southern gentleman and a badass!"

I can feel my face turning into a cherry tomato. Before I can unfreeze my blank stare, the girl with wavy blond hair and electric eyes approaches with a flirtatious smile.

Standing five feet tall and wearing a low-cut shirt that hugs her curves, she extends her hand. "Hi, I'm Jackie."

I suck at being smooth but manage to shake her hand and blurt out, "Nice to meet you."

With awkward handshakes, I introduce myself to the other three women, but they're all drunk and high and don't cringe at my social skills. Brianne, Alex's girlfriend, is tall with pleasant curves on all sides. Peter's fiancé, Noel, is much shorter than Brianne but looks athletic. Tiffany reminds me of Jackie but with brown hair. These women belong on the cover of a magazine.

"Let's ride," Alex says. "It's already eight-thirty. The table's booked for nine, and that thing cost me a pretty penny to reserve."

"You sure Miles is working?" Peter asks.

"Yeah. He's waiting on us."

"Which car we taking?" Peter asks.

"The Escalade. Duh!" Alex says. "What else you think's gonna hold everyone? Just make sure you grab the dab rig and oil."

Peter disappears inside the house while the rest of us pile into Alex's black limited-edition Escalade. I climb into the third row and wedge myself into the back corner. Jackie sits next to me, pressing her small body against mine. Noel slides into our row, pushing Jackie even closer. Geo sits in front of me, with Tiffany and Brianne to his right.

Alex rolls down the driver's window. "Hurry up, Peter Pan! Let's move!"

Peter runs through the front yard with something in his hand. He hops into the passenger seat and closes the door. Now that we're all confined in the car, the smell of alcohol on everyone's breath is obvious. Riding with a drunk driver through crowded Miami streets on a Saturday night seems like a horrible idea.

Alex shifts into reverse and mashes the accelerator. He slams on the brakes, turning us all into bobblehead dolls. Before we can recover from the first whiplash, the SUV accelerates forward. He's driving like a madman, and we haven't even made it off his street. But, no one in the car seems to mind.

These rich college kids are reckless. The whole situation is giving me anxiety, but Jackie's hand on my leg keeps me calm.

"Bust out the rig!" Alex yells to Peter.

"Yeah, P. Pan," Geo says with a playful push of Peter's shoulder. "Let's get baked!"

"Hold up, you damn burnouts." Peter messes with something on his lap. "I'm getting it ready."

Peter leans around his seat and hands Geo a bong attached to what looks like a video game controller, along with a fanny pack. Geo pulls a small jar from the pack and uses a thin metal rod to scrape the sides of the container. What comes out looks like a ball of ear wax, which I'm guessing is concentrated marijuana oil. Even though I've had some wild nights out with friends in high school, I've never smoked weed. I didn't want it to hinder my performance on the range or in the gym.

The electric bong has a screen on it that reads 350 degrees. Geo inserts the wax into the bong and inhales from the mouthpiece. After a few seconds, he exhales a cloud of smoke that fills the entire car. It doesn't smell like weed, though.

"Yew! This thing is ripping!" He tries handing the robot bong to me.

"Nah, man, I'm good for now. Imma stay sober tonight, in case we need a DD."

"Sober my ass!" Geo's eyes are red and watering. "Dude, tonight's your night. We're getting you lit up!"

"I'm good, man. I'll probably have a few drinks at the club."

"Not if you're only nineteen," Alex says. "You can't drink in the club. You gotta get high!"

"Yea, dude!" Geo says. "C'mon! Isn't this your first time smoking? What better time to pop your cherry than tonight?"

The girls are staring at me like I'm a little kid walking into kindergarten. The last thing I want to do is look boring to Jackie. My gut is telling me to stay sober, but the peer pressure is too much.

"Fine." I hold my hand out. "Give me the bong, then, ya psycho."

"Hell yeah! It's called a dab rig, Karen." Geo hands it back to me. "All your complaints to the manager are about to be null and void!"

"You're smoking rosin," Peter says. "Don't waste any. That's strong shit and really expensive!"

"All right, just give me a small hit, then. I don't know how to work this thing."

"I'll work it for you," Geo says. "All you gotta do is pull from the mouthpiece and make sure you hold it in." He scrapes the wax with the metal rod. "This rosin won't make you cough that bad. It's more like water vapor than actual smoke."

Figuring that water vapor can't be that bad, I decide to inhale as long as possible to impress Jackie. Geo puts the rig's mouthpiece to my lips. The crackling sound of the wax burning is followed by a thick cloud rushing into and drying out my throat. My lungs reach full capacity, and a burning sensation causes me to cough uncontrollably. I try to cover my mouth, but I'm oozing saliva everywhere.

Peter passes back a napkin. Everyone in the car is laughing as hard as I'm coughing. It sounds like I have earmuffs on, their laughter slow and muffled. The lights coming from outside the car melt together. I don't think I'm supposed to feel like this after just one hit. My racing heartbeat sounds like it's coming from inside my head.

Geo snaps me out of my trance. "Ease up, champ! Take another hit!"

I push the bong away, still trying to slow my cough. Jackie scratches my back with her nails and runs her other hand through my hair, giving me goosebumps.

"Jake, you high enough back there?" Alex asks.

"Feeling some type of way," I mutter, trying to sound casual. I don't want them to know how high I really am. The city lights are inside the car, dancing between the seats. I'm hallucinating.

"Yeah?" Alex asks. "Eat the chocolate I just gave Geo! It'll keep you lifted after the dab wears off."

The last thing I need is weed. "Nah, man. I'm good. I'm plenty high."

"You have to," Alex demands. "The rosin's gonna wear off! Edibles keep you higher longer."

Jackie's smile is intoxicating. She's definitely the hottest girl I've ever had the chance to be with. I figure I'm already high and you can't overdose on marijuana.

"All right, hand it to me," I tell Geo. "It's just weed, right?"

Geo puts a small ball of chocolate in my hand. "Dude, it's strictly weed."

The edible doesn't taste that bad, despite a bitter aftertaste.

"Did you eat it?" Alex yells back. "Jake? Was it good?"

"It's gone."

"Nice!" Alex says. "Just a heads-up, but there might have been some magic mushrooms in there too."

"What? Don't mess with me like that, man. Come on."

Everyone in the car is giggling. I can't believe these assholes just tricked me.

Geo turns back with a wink and smiles. "You're gonna be fine. I'm looking out for you tonight. Let's have some fun."

I nod and return the smile, feeling a little safer. Jackie's running her nails up and down my arm. Looks like I'm along for this wild ride—no going back. Alex turns up the music and continues down the busy, three-lane road.

We're almost to the bridge that takes us over the Biscayne Bay into Miami Beach. Alex's driving gets more erratic with every turn. He and his friends keep taking hits from a vaporizer pen filled with cannabis, and loud music pulses out of the Escalade's speakers, my head pounding along with the rhythm of the bass. If Jackie weren't touching me, I wouldn't even be on this planet.

"Your skin is so soft," Jackie whispers into my ear, her delicate fingers running up and down my forearm. "I love it. Are you gonna dance with me tonight?"

I nod and smile at her.

Her lips swipe my ear lobe ever so lightly. "Good."

Jackie's warm breath sends chills down my spine, and the hair on the back of my neck is standing at attention. Being this high magnifies every little detail, her voice the sexiest thing I've ever heard.

We approach the top of the causeway, and bright buildings appear. The sheer size of the cityscape is impressive; its overwhelming lights reflect magnificent colors off the massive bay.

It would be much easier to enjoy the sights if Alex weren't swerving so recklessly through traffic, going eighty miles per hour down to forty, then back to eighty. He veers into the far-right lane and speeds up, turning us into bobbleheads yet again.

A small sedan blocks our path several car lengths ahead. Alex looks to make his next move back to the middle lane. At the same time, a black Ford F-350 in the far-left lane is merging into the middle.

I shout, "Look out, dude!"

Alex turns the wheel violently to the right, setting off an uproar of beeping horns. The Ford continues into the middle lane and speeds down the bridge. Everyone in the car is frozen, except for Alex, who continues veering around cars.

"You good back there?" Alex yells, clearly pissed. "I mean, really, man. What the hell? I saw the guy coming!"

He's lying, but it's not worth arguing.

"Sorry," I say. "I just panicked."

"I don't know if you smoked too much weed, or not enough." Alex passes something back. "Here, hit the vape."

"Can I hit it after you?" Jackie asks.

Getting higher is a bad idea, but I just made a fool of myself in front of her. I take a small hit from the vape and even that makes me cough.

Jackie takes the pen and proceeds to make me look like the virgin I am. The cloud of vapor she blows out fills up the entire car, the lights dancing through it.

The buildings along A1A are magnificent, the sidewalks packed with people. Even in twenty-mile-per-hour traffic, Alex is still speeding. Without using his turn signal, he cuts to the left and crosses two lanes of oncoming traffic. Another serenade of car horns follows.

We pull into a parking lot that is something to behold—the Fly High Resort. I've only seen hotels this nice in pictures online. We circle around a large fountain covered in colorful lights, reminding me of the casinos in Las Vegas, and slide into the valet parking line. Within a minute of stopping, a well-dressed man greets us and takes the keys from Alex.

Jackie holds my arm as we follow the group through huge, glass doors with golden handles into the massive lobby with its wall-length mirrors tripping me out. If it weren't for her, being this high in such a crowded place would have already overwhelmed my senses. We get to the elevators, but there are three different sets. The first four cars are for the privately owned condos, the next four used by hotel guests. Past those are two with a glowing "Club Eleven" sign above them.

The line to ride the elevators has got to be at least fifty people long. Alex struts right past everyone, skirting yellow WET FLOOR signs where someone dropped a bottle, and approaches the security guard, drawing a sea of angry looks. The large, tattooed man in all black has a grizzly beard, making him look like a pissed-off Viking.

"Paulsen, Alex Paulsen," Alex says, sounding like he owns the place. "We've got a table reserved for nine o'clock."

"Cool story, buddy," the bouncer says, looking over Alex's shoulder like he's not even there. "You'll have to talk to someone once you get upstairs."

Alex's smirk turns upside down. "Okay, well, which elevator's for VIPs?"

"These two are for everybody. You see that line behind you? You should get in the back of it before it gets longer."

"You're tripping, man. Let me speak to your boss. Miles. It's already five minutes to nine, and I didn't drop ten grand on a table to stand in line!"

The bouncer puffs his chest out and gets in Alex's face. "Not my problem, asshole. You gotta stand in line, like everybody else."

Geo steps in front of Alex and puts his arm out to keep him back. "Relax, Alex. I'm sure everything's gonna be cool. Sir, can we speak to your supervisor? Miles?"

"You can speak to my nuts. If you booked your table at nine, then you shoulda gotten here early enough to stand in line." He presses his hand to Geo's chest and pushes him back.

Geo slaps his hand away. "The last thing you wanna do is touch me, bitch!"

The bouncer takes a step back and squares up like a boxer. Jackie's nails dig into my arm. She's shaking and starting to cry.

*****

Geo's tough, but this guy will crush him. I have to help him fight the bouncer. Turn to page 30.

Get Peter to help me pull the girls back to safety. Turn to page 39.

I'm not going to murder someone by smashing their head in with a bottle, but I can't let this security guard get his ass kicked because he's protecting us. I slide forward and throw my jab at the biggest of the bunch who's raining down punches on JD. The blow knocks his head back and gets him turning toward me just in time to eat my right hand.

The guy stumbles back, but I leap with my left hook and put his punk ass on the ground.

Geo and Alex exchange punches with two of the other men, but Alex is on the losing end of his battle. I grab the guy by his shirt and toss him on his ass, but something pierces my low back over and over before I can react.

I spin around and face the woman. Blood covers her hand.

"Pinche puto!" she says, spitting at me as she backs up.

The pain hits me hard as warm blood spills down my pants. I can't see what she stuck me with, but my hand bumps into the handle of a knife.

"That bitch stabbed me," I say to myself, holding onto the couch to keep my balance.

Geo's trying to fight two of the men, and Alex is nowhere to be seen. Geo lands a nice shot on the big guy, but the dude I had knocked down is back on his feet, holding the tequila bottle by the neck.

I try to warn Geo, but it's too loud and I've barely got enough strength to hold myself up, my shoe soaked in blood.

The guy swings the bottle and shatters it across Geo's head, dropping him to the ground. He points the jagged end at me.

"I'm sorry," I say, my voice barely a whisper, my eyes having a hard time staying open.

He curses me and throws an uppercut with the bottle, the glass blasting into my chin.

***

Try again. Turn to page 38.

I don't like the idea of Geo fighting this monster alone, but he's a big boy and can take care of himself. I ease Jackie behind me and tell Peter, "Help protect the girls."

Peter gets beside me, and we back the girls up as Geo and the bouncer face off.

A security guard in a fancy black suit sprints our way. He jumps between them before a punch is thrown. "What the hell's going on here?" he shouts at the bouncer.

The bouncer starts to answer, but Alex cuts him off. "Miles, your mongoloid here isn't too keen on customer service!"

Miles turns back to the bouncer. "Were you being a problem for my VIPs?"

The tattooed man turns from a Viking warrior into a cat caught in the jaws of a Pitbull. "Sir, I—"

Miles isn't as big as the bouncer, but he's no small man. His defined jawline and serious demeanor make him quite intimidating. "*Were you* being a problem for *my* VIPs?"

"I-I didn't know they were VIPs."

"Bullshit," Alex says. "I told him we had a table reserved right when I walked up!"

Miles shakes his head at the bouncer. "You're fired. Pack your shit and go home."

The man stares back in disbelief. He lowers his eyes to the floor and walks away, mumbling. Another large security guard steps in to take his place. Jackie and the girls are calming down, although the marks on my arm from her nails are still there.

Miles gives Alex a handshake and half hugs him.

Geo greets him the same way, then the security guard turns to me. "Miles—good to meet you. Sorry for my employee's attitude."

"No worries, man. I'm Jake, Geo's cousin."

"Awesome. Any family of Geo is family of mine. I'll make sure you guys have a good time tonight."

After greeting Peter and the girls, Miles walks us to an empty elevator. The walls are made of marble and adorned with beautiful artwork. I'm high enough that my night of fun could be just sitting in here, staring at the designs.

"I'll ride up with you guys to make sure there's no more hiccups," Miles says when the elevator door shuts behind him.

"Sorry to cause all the trouble, but your boy was tripping," Alex says. "I asked for you right away, and he told us to speak to his nuts."

"We just hired that moron. I figured there's no way he can mess up elevator duty. Obviously, not the case."

The elevator ascends. Jackie's holding my arm, her other hand under my shirt. I put my back to the wall and breathe in her beauty while her nails glide across my stomach.

"When he pushed me, it was officially on," Geo says. "If you hadn't gotten there in time, he was gonna get smoked!"

"Speaking of smoked..." Alex pulls the vape pen out of his pocket and hands it to Miles.

"I'm good right now, man. I gotta work till seven." Miles turns and surveys me and the girls. "While I'm thinking about it, is anyone in your group under twenty-one?"

"Ah, really man?" Geo says. "You're gonna give 'em the red wrists of shame?"

"Dude, I have to. Part of the job. I know it sucks, but it is what it is." He pulls red paper bracelets from his jacket pocket. "Okay, who needs one?"

Being underage sucks. Even in the shooting world, people lack respect for me because of how young I am. At least Jackie's in the same boat at eighteen. I reach my right wrist out next to Jackie's so Miles can brand us with the bracelets.

The elegant designs all over the elevator are captivating, moving like an old-timey cartoon. The oil pen comes to Jackie. She takes a massive hit and passes it to me. I feel a bit more comfortable taking a hit now we're not potential victims of Alex's reckless driving. This hit's not as big and way easier on my throat. I pass the pen to Geo and put my arm back around Jackie. The elevator door opens, and loud music floods in from the club. There's over a hundred people standing in line outside a set of doors under the glowing neon sign: "Club Eleven."

Miles escorts us past the entire line, the music punching me in the face when we walk through the door. A DJ is shaking his dreadlocks in circles and spinning the turntables. His booth is surrounded by a circular dance floor filled with a sea of people.

For a room with a thousand lights, it's still very dark, and I almost don't see Miles leading us in the other direction. The flashes and loud noises make it difficult to keep up with the group. It's so crowded, I trip over a stranger's foot and barely catch myself from falling. Different colors linger in front of my eyes, and my stomach's all queasy. This must be the mushrooms kicking in.

Miles stops at a large table with a half-moon couch covered in red leather cushions. He points to it and herds us in like animals.

Sitting down first is probably my best option. Both my legs feel covered in a hundred pounds of candle wax. Jackie sits her perky butt right on my lap. I adjust my pants to keep her from feeling what she's doing to me.

"You guys enjoy!" Miles yells over the music. "I gotta get back to the grind!" He shakes Alex's hand one more time before walking toward the entrance.

Alex shouts something to a tall brunette waitress walking by in an electric blue bikini and bunny ears.

She smiles at him and continues on her way, strutting her stuff and shaking a fluffy tail. The next song starts and the waitress is back, handing a bottle of tequila to Alex. He throws her a wad of cash and opens the bottle while Geo grabs shot glasses from the table. Tiffany hands two shot glasses to Jackie, who hands one to me.

Adding alcohol to the list of drugs I'm on is probably *not* a great idea.

Geo leans over to Jackie and me. "Get down below the couches with those red wristbands of yours!"

Jackie smiles and nods, then pulls me to the floor with her. We crouch on our knees behind the couch, and she yells, "Cheers!"

We toast the shot glasses and down our tequila. The burning sensation in my throat is terrible, but I cringe through it with a smile. Jackie leans in and kisses me, our tongues delicately dancing around each other, until she pulls away with a grin. I'm at a loss for words, and my mouth is still tingling. There's no hiding what's happening under my zipper.

She leans into my ear, gives it a little nibble. "Wanna go dance?"

I'm not saying no to anything she asks for, so I follow her to the hardwood floor. The multicolored lights swirl all around me, my body prickling like I'm plugged into an outlet. It's hard not to trip over all the people when my feet are numb and the bass of the electric music is rattling my entire body and brain.

The dance floor begins with a wall of people moving to the beat, like they're in a trance, and Jackie pulls me into the fray. We find a small space in the middle of all the sweaty bodies. My long legs make for an awkward dance partner, and being this high isn't helping. Jackie takes control, reaching around and placing my hands on her hips. All I can do is try my best to relax and follow her rhythm.

Geo and Tiffany's smiling faces pop out of nowhere. He yells, "You straight, J-Bone?"

I nod with a smirk, even though I'm the furthest thing from straight, my mind crooked from the mushrooms and weed.

Tiffany whispers something into Jackie's ear that makes them giggle. Jackie turns around and wraps her arms around my neck, keeping us dancing next to Geo and Tiffany.

Jackie kisses me again, this time much more intensely, my tongue struggling to keep up. Someone bumps us, and I fall backward into a woman, causing both of us to hit the floor. Jackie stumbles but stays up.

I pop to my feet and try to help the woman stand. She slaps me in the face and screams at me in Spanish.

A large man with a Cuban flag on his dress shirt jumps in front of me. "Qué bola, yuma?" the man yells, spit flying all over my face. "You think you can push a lady like that?"

My heart is racing. "I didn't mean—"

Geo steps in between us. "Relax, amigo, it was an accident."

The Cuban pushes Geo, who returns with a straight right hand and left hook. Both punches land flush on the Cuban's jaw, sending him crashing down, his head bouncing off the hard floor.

The woman tries to help him, but he's dazed.

Geo grabs me by the arm. "Let's go!"

We escape with the girls through the mob of dancing zombies. No one seems to notice a fight just took place over the blaring music. I hope Geo knows where our table is because I can't remember which way to go, my senses completely overloaded. My only focus is clearing the way for Jackie, who's clinching my wrist like she's hanging onto the edge of a cliff.

Geo turns a quick left into our booth and says, "Dude! I just laid this guy out flat! He wanted that smoke!"

"No way!" Alex sets his drink on the table. "Bullshit!"

Geo looks at me. "Tell this idiot who wasted that dude!"

I nod and manage to smile. Alex laughs and grabs the bottle of tequila.

"Why'd you hit him?" Peter asks.

"He got in Jake's face and pushed me, so I two-pieced his ass!"

Alex fills the shot glasses and hands them out. "Celebratory shots for our 'Knockout of the Night' winner!"

Jackie and I duck and throw back the liquor, prompting loud cheers from the boys. I try to stand, but Jackie grabs my arm and kisses me again.

Tiffany interrupts by handing Jackie a vape pen. She inhales for at least ten seconds and then passes it off to me. I take a much smaller hit and puff out a tiny cloud that looks like a spring storm compared to Jackie's hurricane. Geo hits it next.

Colors are leaving the lights and coming toward me. I'm not certain of what's real anymore.

There's a constant vibration coming from my leg, and it's making my heart race. What's going on?

Oh, my phone.

Someone's trying to call me. I pull it out, the screen lighting up with missed calls and group texts to me and Geo from Uncle Shawn.

Where r u guys?

Call me back.

Where'd you guys go?

What's Alex's address?

My phone registers a new text. *Did u leave his house? Call me.*

Uncle Shawn never panics like this. Another one comes through: *Get ur asses back home now!*

Geo's staring down at his phone, shaking his head. He looks up and we lock eyes. I hold my phone out, wondering if he read the texts. Geo shrugs his shoulders, appearing irritated.

That crazy-looking woman tackling the racoon. Holy shit. She was one of them and so close to the house.

Jackie wraps her arms around me from behind and sticks one of her hands down my pants. My clouded mind shifts directions when she pulls me onto the red leather sofa. Alex brings over more shots of tequila, and we drink them down, not even bothering to hide below the couch.

My phone vibrates again. It's an Emergency Alert: *ALL PERSONS WITHIN MIAMI-DADE COUNTY MUST EVACUATE THE COUNTY IMMEDIATELY. IF YOU ARE UNABLE TO DO SO, SHELTER IN PLACE. REMAIN IN YOUR HOMES UNTIL AUTHORITIES SAY OTHERWISE.*

I lock my phone and slide it back in my pocket. Uncle Shawn was probably right. It has to have something to do with the bath salt attacks.

"Hey!" yells an angry voice.

We turn to see a huge man in a black "Club Eleven Security" shirt towering over us. He leans in close and says, "Mind showing me your wrist?"

I'm frozen in place. This dude's a beast.

The bouncer grabs my right arm and inspects the red bracelet. His grip strength is impressive.

Alex steps between me and the bouncer. "What's the problem here, sir?"

"You idiots are giving alcohol to minors over here—that's my problem."

"These guys aren't drinking!"

"You're telling me I didn't just watch these two take a shot?"

"You're tripping, tough guy," Alex tells him.

The security guy stares Alex down. "It's dark in here, but I ain't blind, asshole!"

Geo's behind Alex, both with their fists clinched. I'm close to suffocating from the tension, and the drugs in my system aren't making my thoughts any calmer.

Out of the darkness, several bald men wearing Cuban flag designs on their clothes approach our table. Their large statures, bald heads, and burly beards make them a scary bunch. The man Geo dropped is with them, his girlfriend helping him walk.

My heartbeat is actually hurting my chest from the inside.

The woman points at us and shouts something in Spanish, then transitions to English. "The puto in the white shirt with flowers on it!" she yells, pointing at Geo.

The bouncer turns to them with a puzzled look.

Suddenly, the music comes to a halt, and solid LED lights flash on. The club is almost completely silent, everyone covering their eyes from how bright it's become.

The DJ's voice booms over the loudspeaker. "Everybody, evacuate the club immediately. There's an order to evacuate Miami-Dade County! Please evacuate the club slowly and safely!"

Everyone in the club's looking at their phones, the panic building, tension so high I can feel it crawling on my skin.

The bouncer places his meaty arm between us and the angry group. "All right, everybody, let's go! All of you gotta get out!"

"JD, we got some business to handle," says one of the Cuban men, who obviously knows the security guard.

"Sorry, Jorge, but you're not handling anything here."

Jorge gives him the side eye. "JD, don't get involved. It'll be quick."

The man Geo knocked out interrupts. "Fuck that, let's beat this dude's ass!"

The men attempt to get around JD's tattooed arm to go for Geo, but JD moves his large frame in the way. The dude with the black eye swings a wide left hook at JD, who blocks it and counters with his own left hook, dropping him. The back of his head slams the floor with force.

The gang swarms JD with a barrage of punches coming from all sides, the commotion panicking the crowd. A stampede erupts, people trampling over one another to get to the exit. I don't know if we should flee or save JD. He might end up trying to fight us for starting this whole problem. Maybe we should just leave him to distract our attackers while we escape.

*****

Use a jab, right cross, left hook against the closest guy.
Turn to page 29.

Run to the exit. I've got to get the girls out of here.
Turn to page 135.

Grab the bottle of tequila and use it as a weapon.
Turn to page 42.

I'm done with bullies and want to prove myself to Jackie. I shake her off my arm and push the bouncer as hard as I can.

And his big ass barely moves. He rockets a right hand into my face and my nose crunches.

Geo and Alex rush past me and attack the bouncer, and someone grabs me from behind. I try to fight back but can barely see with my eyes watering from the punch.

Everyone's shouting and screaming. I lose sight of Geo, and I'm so high I can't tell what's going on.

"You're out of here," the guy pulling me says.

I break his grip and spin to face him, see he's more security. I fire a punch, but he's faster and shoves my chest.

My calves knock something over as I backpedal, trying not to fall on my ass. It clatters on the ground, the yellow plastic just visible when my foot flies out from underneath me on the slick tile.

I reach out for Geo, for Jackie, for someone to hold onto, but no one's there. I fall hard, the back of my head whacks the ground with a loud crack.

My sight is gone, my head pounding like it's getting crushed in a vice. I try to sit up, but can't, my hands useless, my leg twitching out of control.

"Jake! Jake!" a girl screams. "Oh shit, his head! He's bleeding! Help!"

***

The correct choice was to get Peter to help me pull the girls back to safety. Turn to page 30.

Peter can't save Noel, but I might be able to. "Hold on," I yell, starting back up the rope.

Noel's screaming at Peter to let her go and Geo's shouting at me to stay the fuck down.

I keep going like I'm back in high school PE and trying to be first to reach the gym's roof.

They continue struggling above me, and I'm swinging on the rope, barely passing the fourth-floor landing. I've got to hurry. "Just hang on," I shout, ignoring the burning in my muscles.

"Jake," Geo shouts. "Get down! The sheets can't handle it."

But I've got to try. She'll die from that high of a fall.

Peter's yelling at Noel to stop as I reach the fifth floor, her kicking feet nearly close enough to grab.

"No!" Peter yells.

I look up at Noel who's falling right for me, her shriek so loud.

There's no time to move out of the way and she slams into my head, knocking me off the rope.

"Oh fuck!!!" I shout as my world turns upside down. I crash into the edge of the fire escape, shattering my shoulder, and fall the wrong way, the ground flying at my face.

***

The correct choice was to let Peter handle Noel.
Turn to page 73.

The guy's got his finger curled around the trigger and probably going to blast us no matter what to get rid of witnesses. I've got the longest reach and he's aiming at Alex. It's up to me.

Knowing it takes a split second longer to squeeze a trigger if you're talking, and not willing to let Alex eat a bullet if I mess up, I ask, "Can I pay you?"

The man starts to say no and I'm in motion, both hands reaching for the gun. I miscalculate the distance, and he shrinks back against the wall, my fingers barely grazing the barrel.

Pop! Pop! Pop! Pop! Click.

I'm blown back against the wall, sliding down it until I'm shoulder to shoulder with JD whose head is slumped over. Geo and Alex are beating the gunman, the girls screaming for help, but it will never come in time for me, blood spurting out the holes in my chest.

***

The correct choice was to talk the situation down.
Turn to page 99.

I search for alternate exits away from the hurricane of alarmed people, but there aren't any. We need JD to show us a way out of here. The drugs and alcohol in my system aren't making this choice any easier.

I snatch the half-empty tequila bottle off the table. One of the men beating JD pulls out a knife and raises it, but before he can stab anyone, I swing the bottle at his head as hard as I can. It's a home run. The bottle shatters across his bald skull, spraying tequila and blood on everyone. He collapses to the floor, out cold.

Geo and Alex put fists on the others still pummeling JD. I grab the behemoth by the collar of his security shirt and drag him out of the fray. He gets to his feet while wiping blood from his face. Alex and Geo stand back up after finishing off the final two men. Everyone who attacked us is lying unconscious on the floor. The woman tries to wake them and screams hysterically in Spanish.

Both visible exits are completely blocked by screaming crowds trying to tear each other apart. The girls are all crying.

Jackie clutches me tightly. "What are we going to do?"

"I know a way out!" JD yells. "Follow me!"

None of us hesitate. We sprint across the deserted dance floor, jump over the bar, and run through the kitchen. JD pulls out a bundle of keys and unlocks the door at the very back.

"Where are we going?" Brianne asks.

Alex strokes her hair. "We're finding an exit. We're going to be fine."

Jackie's nails dig into my arm again. The door opens into a long hallway. We follow JD like a line of ducklings behind their mother, approaching another door at the end of the hall. This time, the doorway leads into a stairwell. Chaotic screams and slamming doors echo from below, like everyone is trying to escape at the same time.

JD looks to us. "The parking lot's right below us. Did you valet your car?"

Alex nods.

"Then all our cars are down there. We've got eleven floors to descend. Let's go!"

I can't stop staring through all the stairs to the first floor below. The height makes me dizzy. Eleven floors never seemed so high. I grab the handrail to keep from falling over, still extremely high and drunk.

"Yo!" Geo grabs me by the collar and spins me around. "You good? Let's get the hell out of here!"

We rush after the group, who's already a dozen stairs in front of us. The further down we get, the louder the chaos becomes. We pass the tenth floor, then the ninth. My anxiety is making it difficult to breathe.

Alex and Peter push JD to go faster as we pass the eighth floor. Brianne slips in her high heels and falls on the landing with a loud thud, bursting into tears. Alex helps her up, but she can't put any weight on her right ankle.

The girls are in full panic mode, eyeliner and mascara running down their faces. The rest of us aren't doing much better.

JD continues to lead the others, while Geo and I help Brianne onto Alex's back. We pass the seventh floor and are nearly to the sixth when the sound of gunfire freezes us.

Pop! Pop! Pop!

It's coming from inside the stairwell, coupled with blood-curdling screams. The shots are extremely loud, making my chest vibrate. It sounds like a handgun, but we're not sticking around to find out.

JD grabs his keys and unlocks the door to the sixth floor. "Hurry!" he yells, pushing us into the hallway.

Many of the condo doors are wide open, clothes and personal belongings scattered about on the floor. Everyone's frantic, scrambling to get out of the building. We pause at the next intersection for a split-second, long enough to see a mass of people jostling for position in front of the elevator. Alex looks winded from carrying Brianne, and nobody in the group seems to know where to go.

I pull my phone out to do some quick research, but before I can type in my passcode, a metal door to our left swings open and slams against the wall. A thin man in plaid pajamas and glasses darts out of the room and collides with JD. The small man's glasses go one way, and he flies the other, landing flat on his back. JD, who gets knocked into the wall, becomes enraged. He grabs ahold of the frail man, wrapping both hands around his throat.

Pop! Pop! Pop! Pop!

After the first bang, all I hear is ringing. JD goes limp and falls backward, his hands clutching his bloody chest.

What nobody saw was the subcompact pistol in the man's hand. He gets up, presses his back against the wall, and points the gun at us, silencing our screams. Our hands go up. His aim wavers between Alex and Peter, who are closest to him. We're at the mercy of a man in blood-splattered, plaid pajamas.

I've been around guns my whole life but never had one aimed at me. My arms are sky-high, same as everyone else.

The man's gaze goes from Alex to Geo, me then Peter, his pocket pistol steadied between us. He's only got three or four rounds left, but all he needs is one to take another life.

"Stay back," he says, his voice shaking.

*****

Distract him and grab the gun. Turn to page 41.

Talk the situation down. Turn to page 99.

There have got to be close to a hundred keys scattered on the ground, but less than a dozen with Dolphin keychains. I hate the idea of trying to carjack someone, so I hand Geo the revolver and tell him, "Cover me. I'll find the key."

He takes the gun. "I don't know. We still gotta find the car."

I'm on my knees tossing the useless keys to the side. "We'll find it. We gotta."

"Oh fuck. Hurry up."

I toss aside a Toyota key and a Tesla, relieved when I find one for an Escalade. "Got it," I say, getting to my feet.

Blam! Blam!

The revolver fired just inches from my left ear, and both of mine ring so loud I can't hear what Geo's shouting. But that doesn't stop me from chasing after him and away from the pack of crazed people he just shot at.

Geo turns into the parking lot and veers left at the valet sign. "Hit the button!" he screams in my face.

I hit the lock button over and over, keeping an eye out for flashing brake lights and hoping Geo might hear it over the rest of the chaos.

Geo skids to a stop, but I don't see the Escalade anywhere. He raises the revolver and fires two shots at the pack of rabid people pouring through the cars to our right. Two of the people drop, but at least a dozen more pour forward.

"Go!" he screams, firing his last bullet before taking off after me.

I run between two SUVs on my left and glance back at Geo. My leg slams into a low hanging chain and I fly onto the pavement, scraping the skin off my palms.

Geo grabs my arm and jerks me to my feet, but the rabid people are right behind him, tackling us both to the ground.

"Get the fuck off me!" Geo shouts.

I push one off before it bites my face, but its friends are clawing at my arms, pinning them down, tearing at my neck, my chest, my legs, everything on fire.

***

Try again. Turn to page 76.

I don't give a damn if I get disqualified. Ain't no one talking shit about my father, a man who gave all he had for his country.

I take another step toward Blevins, forcing him to crane his head back to look me in the eyes. Lowering my voice so no one else can hear, I say, "Look here, you little fuck. Unlike you, I don't need a gun to prove I'm a man. You ever say another word about my father, and I will break every goddamn bone in your body."

Blevins steps back, putting his chin in perfect range for a right hook, but he raises his hands, chickening out just like I knew he would. "It was a joke," he says.

"Yeah, well that shit ain't funny."

He nods and walks away probably figuring he doesn't need to get embarrassed by me twice in one day.

Geo claps me on the back. "Good shit, J-Dog. I thought I was gonna have to wreck that son of a bitch."

I unclench my fists and turn to Geo. "And I know you would've."

Uncle Shawn's talking to one of the officials by the winners' podium. He spots me as I trot over and claps me on the back. "So proud of you, stud!" he says. "Roger, this is my nephew, Jake Swisher. Jake, this is Roger Hersh, the head of Sig's competition team."

A sponsorship from SIG would be amazing. Trying not to sound too excited, I say, "Hello Mr. Hersh. It's great to meet you."

"Please, call me Roger," he replies with a smile. "It's great to meet you, Jake. I saw your final run. Stage three's no joke, and you finished without penalties. That's impressive. If I'm not mistaken, you broke Blevins' record."

I stumble over my words like a fanboy. "Yes, sir. I—"

A yell from Blevins cuts me off. "Are you serious?" he shouts at the two police officers placing him into handcuffs. "Everybody here knows me! I'm no threat to anyone!"

Judging by the scrunched look on the cops' faces, they can smell Lionheart's rotten teeth. "Sir, you can't put your hands on an event official. Especially not while holding a firearm. Let's not make this difficult."

"Sorry, guys," Roger says. "I have to deal with this. Talk soon, Shawn!" He jogs toward the unfolding drama.

Uncle Shawn shakes his head at Blevins. "What a shame. The guy just can't keep it together." He pats me on the back. "Come on. Let's go pack up."

Geo's already put my guns in the range bags and loaded them onto our four wheelers. He's waiting for us at the table. "Today can't get any better," he says. "You win first place, and Blevins goes to jail. Hashtag, *blessed*!"

Uncle Shawn cuts off Geo's obnoxious chuckles. "Son, do you really have to go there?"

"What? He deserves it. You're telling me that Scott Blevins doesn't deserve to go to jail?"

"I don't care if he deserves it or not! It looks bad for the range, bad for the event, and most of all... bad for the sport! And now they probably ain't gonna have the awards ceremony. Sorry, Jake. I'll make sure you get your money."

I say thanks and tie down all my bags to the ATVs.

"Who cares?" Geo asks. "We'll have our own celebration."

"Yeah, I'll throw some steaks on the grill back at the house," Uncle Shawn says. "We'll make the most of it."

Geo shakes his head. "Save the red meat and charcoal. Me and my friends will take care of the celebrating."

"That's a big N-O! You and your burnout college buddies ain't corrupting him. He's actually focused, with goals. Sorta like somebody I used to know."

"I'm in school full time!"

"Yeah, tell me about it." Uncle Shawn looks exactly like Dad when he'd had enough of me. "A hundred grand spent on elective classes, and you still can't pick a major. What's your degree gonna be? Partying? Procrastinating? Bullshitting?"

"Sorry, master buzz-killer. Wish I could be mister Navy Seal for ya, or as focused as Jake. Can a man have a little time to find himself in today's world?"

"You ain't a man, son. When you're the one paying to *find yourself,* then you'll be a man."

"Dad, for once, don't give us a hard time. Let us go out. We won't be gone that late." Before Uncle Shawn shuts him down, Geo says, "Jake, you're the champ. Please tell him that you'd like to actually *enjoy* Miami."

Being caught in the middle of their arguments sucks, and picking sides is never a good idea. I've had a long week and even longer day, plus I have a flight back to South Carolina tomorrow morning. A victory steak before going to bed early sounds way more appealing than partying, but I don't want to let Geo down.

Always the peacekeeper, I say, "I mean, a nice night out on the town would be cool. Uncle Shawn, you could come too."

"No way," Geo says. "Master buzz-killer won't come. He doesn't even want *us* going!"

"I ain't going 'cause I got re-*spon-si-bi-li-ties.* I gotta close up shop here and try to save face after Blevins' dumbass fit. I ain't the only one with chores either. You and the champ gotta clean these guns until they look brand new."

"Dad, really? He *just* won the biggest tournament of his life. Can he catch a break? If you let us go out, I'll personally clean all of his guns spotless tomorrow. Deal?"

Uncle Shawn laughs. "That'll be the day. You, clean a gun thoroughly? Yeah, right."

"I'll clean them until you tell me they're perfect. Just let us go out."

"Son, it ain't just that." Uncle Shawn's tone turns serious. "I don't feel comfortable with you going downtown tonight."

"Oh my God! Are you really going to pull the bath salt people out your ass?"

"Geo, have you not seen the reports? Do I really have to explain it to you?"

"No, but I know you're gonna."

"In the last month, there have been over twenty incidents in the Miami area—people behaving like rabid animals, killing innocent victims. Eating them, according to the news articles."

"Probably just more psychos on bath salts," Geo says, pulling out his phone. "Have you seen the videos of these druggies?"

"They ain't druggies, Geo!" Uncle Shawn stares Geo down. "Their toxicology reports came back negative for controlled substances. After that, all the information on them goes dark."

The mainstream media doesn't give the stories much coverage and never mentions the drug tests. On the internet, however, the videos and conspiracy theories have gone viral. It's hard to know what to believe. The attacks are brutal, some even happening in broad daylight. Whether or not they're on bath salts, they really do resemble rabid dogs.

"Watch this!" Geo holds out his phone to show a video. "Oh my God, look at how he just tackles that dude!"

Uncle Shawn turns away in disgust. "You really don't get how serious this is? Me and my colleagues have some theories, and none of them are good. It could be some type of virus or even some kinda genetic mutation."

Geo rolls his eyes and uses his hands to make a triangle on top of his head. "Oh, here we go! Tinfoil-hat man with his flannel-wearing, conspiracy friends are here to save the day!"

"Me and my *flannel* friends know people on the inside of things, and what we're hearing ain't good." Uncle Shawn stuffs a box of ammo into a rifle bag. "You ain't going downtown tonight. I'm telling you, it's not smart!"

"Fine. I'll stay away from the Corona zombies. *But* we're going to Alex's house. He lives west of the interstate. It's only fifteen minutes from here, so it's not *downtown*."

"If I let you go to Alex's, you're cleaning all them guns tomorrow. I'll be watching over you like a hawk. I want every nook and cranny sparkling."

"Deal!" Geo says, smiling over his small victory. He starts the engine on his four-wheeler and nods at me. "Race you to the house?"

Uncle Shawn holds up his hand. "Before you go, are you carrying?"

Geo looks at him like he's crazy. "Right now?"

"Right now. And when you go to Alex's?"

"No, Dad, I'm not. This isn't a war zone. Alex isn't Osama Bin Laden's cousin. So, I think I'm good without carrying a damn gun. Why are you so paranoid?"

"Being prepared isn't paranoid, son. Carry something, please. It'd make me feel better."

"Sure, Dad. Sure." Geo shakes his head and speeds off.

I load the last bag onto my ATV and start the quarter-mile trip back to the house. It's a beautiful ride down a dirt road through the Everglades, with the cool night air cutting through my thin clothing. The south Florida weather in December is amazing—seventy degrees and sunny all day, sixty degrees at night.

After a final bend, the road opens into a football-field-sized yard. From the outside, Uncle Shawn's house looks like an average brick home, but it's way bigger than it appears. Turns out, it's four thousand square feet on the inside.

I park my ATV in the garage next to Geo's and drop off the gear.

We head into the kitchen, and he slams the door shut, making me jump. "Can you believe how paranoid that man is?" he asks. "I didn't even want my concealed weapons permit."

"You didn't want it?"

"No, I couldn't care less. He made me get it when I turned twenty-one. In his head, the guy's still deployed overseas."

"Well, maybe—"

Geo smacks his palms on the kitchen counter. "You know he's got a secret bomb shelter hidden out by the Everglades? He's a psycho!"

"Wait, what? A bomb shelter?"

"Yeah, the thing is made of steel and concrete. I don't know if he thinks the zombies will be carrying nukes or what, but he takes everything too far."

Geo's been known to exaggerate, so it's hard to tell if he's lying about the bomb shelter. I'm actually on Uncle Shawn's side of this dispute, but I can't tell Geo that. "Yeah, man, sucks he rides you so hard. Maybe the Corona zombies'll be flying fighter jets or something. But let's not sweat it. We've got a great night of catching up to look forward to."

"You're right, man." He pulls out his phone. "Let me call Alex and find out tonight's game plan."

"I thought we were just going over to his house to hang out."

Geo quiets me by holding up his finger. "What's up, Alex? What's on the A-list tonight?"

I peel off my sweaty shirt, pretending like I'm not paying attention to the call.

"Yeah? She's coming with her? She meets quality control standards? Well, my cousin's a stud. He ain't jumping on no grenades for the crew."

I take off my shoes and socks, revealing my dry, cracked feet.

"Club Eleven? I'm down for that." Geo paces back and forth. "Wait, you got a table already? Sick! That's money!"

He can't be serious. If Uncle Shawn says it's not safe to go out tonight, then I believe him. My feet look worse than a coal miner's from competing all day. I could just tell Geo I'd rather stay in.

"No, we still gotta get cleaned up. We'll be there *ASAP*." Geo hangs up. "Hey, how fast can you take a shower and not smell like armpits?"

"Why are we in a rush? I thought we were just going to Alex's house?"

"Yeah, we're heading straight to Alex's... and then he's gonna drive us to Club Eleven. Our boy is the head of security there and hooked up a table. We basically own the place."

"You think that's gonna fly with your dad?"

"He ain't gonna find out. I have to take you out for a legit night in Miami. Club Eleven's one of the dopest spots, and the chick I'm dating is bringing one of her hot friends. Alex said she's a dime!"

My gut is telling me this whole thing is a bad idea. On the other hand, I haven't gotten to spend quality time with Geo in a while. I guess I need to loosen up and go along for the ride. It doesn't hurt that a beautiful girl will be there.

I sigh. "All right, just give me a minute."

"Cool, but hurry up. They want us there right now so we can pre-game before we leave. And I don't want Dad to know, so we gotta dip before he gets back."

The whole time I'm in the shower, I hope Uncle Shawn will get home in time to ruin Geo's plans. Then, I can just pretend to be bummed about it and get some rest, but no such luck.

I've just finished drying off when Geo's truck cranks up in the front yard. After throwing on a pair of jeans with a dark red collared shirt, I jump into his freshly washed Tacoma.

Geo's in a bright white button-up shirt with a floral design all over it. He looks obnoxious, like a typical Florida man out for a night in Miami.

My seatbelt barely clicks and we're speeding down the dirt driveway. Uncle Shawn's truck is headed our way, but Geo doesn't even slow down. We turn right onto Swisher Road, the dirt road leading from the family property to the highway. It winds through the woods for over a mile, moss hanging from the tunnel of trees overhead. At night, the road is so dark it's kind of creepy.

"Hey, you hear about the new virus?" Geo asks, breaking the silence. "It's called COVID-4EVER. Only guys in flannel shirts contract it. The symptoms include being a paranoid douche who annoys his kids."

Uncle Shawn seems like a level-headed man who's been through a lot in life. Him and Dad were involved in so many military operations, it's no wonder he's cautious, but I play along.

"Yeah? How do you catch it?"

"If you carry a gun long enough, it'll slowly infect your whole body. At first, you become schizophrenic about drug addicts eating you. Then, you'll start trying to get your family members to carry a gun 'cause crackheads might eat them too! Eventually, you wall yourself off at home, sucking the fun out of everyone around you."

"What do you think's making them go crazy and try to eat people?"

"Dude, it's some new meth or PCP... crack, I don't know. This is Miami, man, drug capital of the U.S. Does it really surprise you that some new drug hits the streets and doctors can't detect it yet?"

That's a fair point. "It's probably just some new form of bath salts or something."

Geo grabs his crotch, a crazy look on his face. "I've got some bath salts right here that are gonna make this chick act rabid tonight."

I give a little chuckle as Geo cracks more jokes. We're turning left onto Highway 41, when he pumps the brakes. There's a raccoon in the road up ahead. He flashes the brights to scare it out of our way.

Something sprints out of the shadows from our left.

A bloody woman in tattered clothes runs across the road, dives on the raccoon, and buries her face in it. Before we react, she takes off into the woods with the animal.

I shout, "What the hell was that?"

"Probably some homeless person looking for dinner," Geo says, his tone shaky and unsure.

"You don't wanna check it out?"

"Nah, dude. We're already going to be late to Alex's. I don't need to go treasure hunting for homeless methheads."

*****

Demand Geo stop the truck to investigate. Turn to page 12.

Follow Geo's lead and don't worry about it. Turn to page 19.

Tiffany is going burn alive if I don't get her out first, and there's no doubt Geo would demand that if he were conscious. I jump into the back, the plastic melting, the flames so hot I can only get close enough to grab Tiffany's feet.

She's wedged in too tight. My pulls do nothing, her hair now on fire. I drop her legs and reach under the seat Alex had been in. My palm burns on the metal handle, but I'm able to drag the seat forward, making some space.

I grab Tiffany's legs again and wrench with all I've got, the fire crisping her forehead, my eyes stinging so bad I can barely keep them open.

One more tug and she finally slides to the floor, so close to the open door that's being licked by the flames. I keep dragging and scream for Geo who's still slumped over.

Boom!

The explosion blows me back into the dashboard, and my forehead feels like it's been split in two as flames engulf the car.

I go to push Geo out the passenger door but am stopped when I turn my head, the pain ten times worse than any migraine. I reach for what hurts and slice my hand on a chunk of metal embedded in my skull, my blood sizzling as the fire takes us.

***

The correct choice was to retrieve Geo before Tiffany.
Turn to page 69.

Hotwiring a car doesn't seem like a fast option. Putting a gun to someone innocent to steal theirs doesn't feel right either.

I yell, "Let's pray one of these abandoned cars has keys in it!"

Geo nods and runs toward the stream of empty vehicles in the middle of the road. I de-cock the hammer on the revolver, replace the empty casing with a fresh round, and sprint after him.

Geo approaches every empty car, peering through the windows, until he reaches a silver Ford Expedition.

"It's still running!" he shouts, jumping in. "And we can fit everyone!"

It's trapped in between several cars. He must still be high. "There's no way you're getting that out of there!"

Geo waves me away, the tires spinning like a drag racer's. He smashes into a convertible, pushing it into the intersection. The Expedition reverses with the same ferocity into a minivan. He cuts a tight U-turn and pulls up beside me.

Geo yells at me, but I can't hear him over the frightened screams of the city.

I throw myself into the passenger seat. Before I close the door, he's already punching the gas. We're speeding down the sidewalk, swerving around debris and fallen people. He slams on the brakes and cuts a hard left down the alley.

Geo turns the high beams on, illuminating our friends hiding behind a dumpster. "Alex!" he shouts out the window. "It's us! It's Geo!"

Alex steps out into the blinding headlights. "Geo! Whose car are you in? Where's mine?"

Geo swings his door open. "Dude, we have to get the hell out of here now!" He runs past Alex to the dumpster where the girls are hiding. "Jake! Open the back of the truck up for Peter and Noel!"

The thought of what happened to my new friends hits me like a sucker punch. I jump out of my seat, open the back of the SUV, and jog over to Geo and Alex to help get everyone into the car. The girls are all sobbing next to Peter and Noel's lifeless bodies. We have to get the girls into the car first. Alex and Geo herd them toward the back passenger door.

Shrieks of anger and pain echo down the dark end of the alley. My hand finds the revolver on my hip. The sound of feet running in our direction is getting louder. Jackie is almost in the car when a snarling woman in a blood-soaked blouse dives out of the shadows and tackles her.

I boot the woman in the face with all my strength, knocking her onto her back. Without hesitation, I draw the revolver and put two bullets in the woman's head. She looks similar to the paramedic I shot earlier, like a rabid animal.

"What the fuck was that?" Alex yells.

Geo dives into the driver's seat. "Just get in! Let's go!"

I help Jackie up and into the car, then dive in behind her, slamming the door shut. A pack of bath salt people are running right for us.

"What about Noel and Peter?" Brianne shouts. "We have to get them!"

The fastest rabid person in front looks like a linebacker, muscles bulging in his bright blue security shirt. He's only a few feet from Geo's door, our engine revving but not moving.

Slam! The bouncer's forehead cracks the window, his body denting the door. A ponytailed woman in leopard print throws herself at a side window, trying to bite through the glass but only managing to knock out her front teeth.

Geo's shaking the gear shift. "Shit!"

Bodies bounce off the car. *Bam! Bam! Bam!*

All of us are screaming, Jackie beyond hysterical. Same for the people battering our car, their bloodthirsty shrieks filled with pain as they break their bones.

I yell at Geo, "Go! Go! Go!"

Geo puts the car in reverse and slams the gas. As we pull away, another rabid person dives onto the woman who attacked Jackie.

Geo yells my name. "Reach back there and close that door!"

The back door swings up and down as we speed in reverse. I climb into the third row of seats and get it closed.

Alex looks at me with wide eyes. "What were those people doing? What are they?"

Geo slams on the brakes and spins us around, aims for the sidewalk. I holster the gun, clutch the seat, and grab the handle.

"Don't stop!" Tiffany shouts. "They're coming!"

Pedestrians scramble out of our way, and we keep going, horn blaring. Geo blasts through a wooden bench and barely misses the light pole. This is insane, but we're just a fraction of the chaos surrounding us, everyone in full hysterics.

Jackie and Tiffany are still screaming in the far back, Brianne right behind me, mumbling, "Holy shit," over and over.

Alex points up ahead. "Go north. Get off the island."

Geo nods, the only one of us keeping cool. We round the corner and nearly hit the group of tough guys in tank tops in the intersection. Geo sticks to the sidewalk because there's a wreck in the road, no cars getting through.

Jackie's freaking out in the backseat. "Get it off me! Get it off."

I spin around, expecting to see her being throttled by a bath salt person, but she's swatting at her hair and cheeks. "I need something for my face," she screams. "It got its—"

"Tiffany," Geo says, somehow keeping cool as we blast by a foot from the storefronts. "Do something about her."

Tiffany pulls a small hand towel from the backseat pocket of the car and hands it back to them. "Here."

Jackie wipes her face, cries with her forehead buried in the hand towel.

The street is clear after the wreck. Geo gets us off the sidewalk and back on the road, punching the gas. I climb into the front seat in case Geo needs help and replace the two empty casings.

"Keep heading north," Alex says.

We're coming up on a road with a sign pointing toward I-95, but it's completely gridlocked with a serenade of horns.

Brianne's sobbing behind me. "Noel and Peter are dead."

Their splats replay in my head, mix with the tearing of flesh, the blood spraying, the bullets punching holes. I'm gonna be sick but can't figure out how to roll the window down. I open the car door a crack.

"Dude, don't!" Geo screams, like he thinks I'm going to jump.

The puke flies out my mouth, splattering the door and the concrete we're flying over. I close it and wipe my mouth with the back of my hand.

Geo doesn't take his eyes off the road. "You cool?"

Alex offers the vape pen. "Here, dog."

"You crazy?"

"You're already high. The pen will help with the nausea."

I guess it makes sense and take a hit from the pen. It gets me coughing, and I'm still nauseous.

Brianne holds up her phone. "Everyone's hashtagging BathSaltPeople and BSP."

Alex has his out too. "People are saying its rabies!"

Traffic jams and abandoned cars are blocking all the roads that will take us across the inter-coastal.

"NBC Miami," Alex says. "If we can't leave Miami County by six a.m., we gotta take shelter."

"It's some type of virus," Brianne adds.

"This one says it's airborne," Alex agrees. "A lot of people are calling bullshit."

"BS about what?" I ask. "This shit's real as hell."

"This conspiracy guy I follow says it's a type of rabies that spreads only by fluid," Alex says.

"Finally." Geo nods at the upcoming road on our left.

I don't see an opening until Geo swerves in front of an oncoming car and into the gas station on the corner, flying over the curb.

We're sailing through the parking lot. There's a family running from the street and between the gas pumps. Ten feet behind them are two rabid bath salt women chasing them.

Geo stomps the accelerator and veers toward the pumps, looking like he's going to run over the family.

*****

Let Geo drive and whatever happens happens.
Turn to page 62.

We can't run over innocent people. Grab the wheel.
Turn to page 116.

We're going way too fast for me to grab the wheel, especially with gas pumps on either side of us. I yell, "Hold on," in case everyone in the back doesn't see what's about to happen.

Geo swerves at the last second, avoiding the family and aiming for the bath salters a few feet from our bumper, no idea what's coming.

The woman with the short blond hair and filthy white scrubs smashes into the windshield, turning my half into a maze of cracks. The long-haired brunette beside her crunches underneath our wheels.

Geo's side of the windshield is clear enough for him to see through, his face stone-cold. He guns the Ford Expedition toward the open street, heading west toward I-95. All of us are silent except for sobs from the back.

We blast off the curb and onto the street, Geo sitting upright, hands at ten and two like he's testing for his license. Just like all the other roads, this one clogs half a block down, our speed down to ten miles an hour.

Geo blows out a breath. "Damn," he says. "Let's hope all parties involved had insurance."

I don't get what Geo's saying, until Alex chuckles. I feel guilty laughing, but it's good to breathe and be alive. "I'm glad you're the one driving."

"Keep on here until we can't move," Alex tells Geo.

"Mom? Mom?" Tiffany says. "Can you hear me?"

She's wiping the tears from her eyes, the phone held to her ear. Jackie's punching numbers on hers.

Brianne asks Alex what she should do.

"You look out that side. Shout if you see any of those bastards."

I'm pulling out my phone and notice my door's unlocked. After pushing down the lock, I warn everyone else to check theirs. "I'd buckle up."

Jackie's bawling. "They won't answer."

"I'm so sorry, Mom," Tiffany says. "I'm scared."

Alex points to the right. "Up there. Take it."

"It's one-way."

"Screw it," Alex says. "This is too slow."

Geo goes for it, sticking to the right side of the street and throwing on his high beams. Fortunately, there are only a few cars on the road—a couple here and there pulling out of their driveways.

"Take this to the end," Alex says. "It'll bring us to the bridge."

My phone is full of missed calls and a dozen texts from Uncle Shawn.

U 2 need 2 get home right now!

Im in the bunker Jake! Hurry! Call me back!

Why arent u picking up?

There r rabid people everywhere and multiplying quick!

Its a virus that spreads fast! Any contact with infected persons bodily fluids and ur fucked!

Where r u guys? U better not be around lots of people!

Its a new form of Lyssavirus. Thats rabies! It doesnt take a bite to spread, just fluid on ur skin!

Its fast acting! Symptoms within 30 minutes! U need 2 call me!

GET TO THE BUNKER NOW!

A horn blares, and a truck blows by us, someone's middle finger sticking out the window. Geo's calm, eyes focused on the road, our speed a safe thirty-five.

"Your dad's been texting like crazy," I tell him. "Sounds pissed."

"Big surprise."

"Two more blocks," Alex says.

"He's saying we got to get home," I tell Geo. "That it's a type of rabies. Not to get it on our skin."

"I plan on it."

"Should I call him back? He sounds worried."

Geo shakes his head. "I don't give a shit. We just need to get over the bridge."

I hit Shawn's number, and he picks up before the first ring ends.

"Where the hell are you guys?" Shawn asks.

Geo takes the next turn, the onramp for the bridge right in front of us.

"On the way home from downtown Miami," I say, embarrassed I sound like a little kid caught being naughty.

"Miami?" he shouts, making me pull back from the speaker. "Miami is a war zone! They might even terminate it! Where are you?"

"We're, umm, going over a bridge."

"Which bridge? The intercoastal? Are you on the way here?"

I'm too high to figure out the name of the bridge, and I don't want to bother Geo. "We're heading to you now," I say, trying to stay calm. "Who are the people we saw? The bath salt people are like zombies!"

"What? You saw them? Did you touch them?" Shawn's never talked like this to me. "Did you touch *those people*?"

"No, but we saw them and ran. Who are they? *What* are they?"

The Honda hatchback in front of us throws on its brakes. Geo swerves, and we barely miss them. They've got a pack of bath salters pounding the hood of their car.

"They're not zombies, and they're not on bath salts," Shawn says. "They're rabid. It's a new form of the lyssavirus that we think came out of the Everglades. It's fast-spreading and fast-acting. You're sure you didn't touch any of those people?"

I look at Jackie, wonder how much of the woman's gross fluid got on her face.

"Are you sure you didn't touch any of them, Jake? What is wrong with you?"

"Nothing. I'm fine. Just scared."

"Let me talk to Geo."

I offer the phone to Geo, but he refuses, his eyes on the road. The street is clogged at the bottom of the bridge. He takes us on the first left and says, "Can't talk."

"He can't talk right now," I tell Shawn. "I'll put him on in a second."

"The hell he can't. Put me on speaker!"

I can't find the speaker button but don't tell him. I just hold the phone between the two of us. "We're trying to get home right now, and it's hell out here," I say, bursting into tears. "Please, help us. So many people are dead, and I don't know... I'm just... I'm just so—"

"Calm down, son. You're gonna be all right. But I need you to listen to me."

"Okay."

"What street are you on right now?"

I look out the passenger window and spot the sign. "We just went over the bridge on One-Sixty-Third Street."

"Okay, I know where you are. Keep making your way west, and be careful when you go past I-95. Take as many back roads as you can."

I try not to sound suspicious when I ask, "What happens if someone gets touched by someone who's infected?"

"If any fluids from an infected person make contact with your skin for more than a second, you're compromised. Within thirty minutes, someone who's been infected will either start having painful headaches, fever, or start itching the site where the fluid touched."

"But you—"

"Shut up and I'll tell ya! The symptoms'll keep getting worse until they start bleeding from their orifices. We've even seen some act like rabid animals for up to three hours before finally dying. The virus attacks the brain stem and spinal column fast but differently in every case."

This can't be real.

"How do you know all of this? Who's *we*? What're you talking about?"

"I've answered enough questions, Get your ass home now."

We're back to crawling at five miles per hour, the sign for US1 up ahead. I tell Shawn, "We're trying to get past all this mess, but there's too much traffic."

Geo grabs the phone out of my hand. "Quit giving Jake shit! I'm trying to get us the hell home, but we're in quite a pickle!"

"Are you serious, you idiot?" Shawn says, yelling so loud it might as well be on speaker. "Where the hell did you go? You realize there's a crisis right now, you burnout! Tell me you're not out partying!"

"Yes, Dad, we were out partying," Geo says sarcastically. "We didn't know all of this was going to happen. What's going on? Explain it instead of yelling at me, for once."

Geo's got the phone to his ear, steering with his left hand. "No, Dad." He listens, then says, "No, not technically."

There's a wreck on the side of the road—a bath salter in blue jeans and a bowling shirt leaning into the front window and chewing on the person in the driver's seat.

"They didn't on purpose," Geo says. "Well, someone we're with got tackled."

Tiffany and Brianne are both on their phones, and Jackie is holding her head and crying.

"It was only for a second, though," Geo says. "No, she's fine." He checks his rearview. "She's fiiiiine."

Alex taps my shoulder. "What's up?" he asks. "What's he saying?"

"We had eight people with us. Now there's only six," Geo says. "We just lost 'em."

I shake my head at Alex and focus on Geo.

"I don't know," Geo says. "We lost sight of where they went. Look, I'm coming, but I'm bringing my friends with me."

"Hell no, you're not!" Shawn shouts.

"Dad, I'm bringing them whether you like it or not."

I pray Shawn doesn't mean me.

"I'm bringing them," Geo says. "Screw you."

"Take the street on the left," Alex says.

Geo veers left, the phone still against his ear, his eyes on fire. We're halfway across the road when headlights flood our car and Geo says, "Shit!"

Boom! Our car spins, and my head smashes the window.

Oh my God. Everything hurts. My eyes are heavy, hard to open. I wipe at them, see the blood on my fingers, flashing blue lights filling our car.

There's a small gash on the side of my head, the passenger window no more. "What the hell happened?"

No one answers.

My vision doubles and blurs, no mistaking the smell of burning gasoline. Geo's head is slumped over, his chin on his chest.

I tilt his head back against the headrest and shake him. "Geo, wake up."

He doesn't respond.

I grab his wrist and check his pulse, not sure if I feel it because I'm still high. His door is blocked by the bulky police car that rammed us. I undo Geo's seatbelt and pull him to my side, throwing open my door.

There aren't any bath salters around, so I check in the back of the car, hoping Alex and the rest can help me get Geo. Alex looks dazed, his eyes staring at the floor. Brianne is right next to him, completely knocked out. There's no sign of Jackie or Tiffany.

The back of the Ford Expedition is scrunched up and filling with smoke. The old-school Mustang we slammed into after being rammed is on fire from the impact.

Tiffany's ass is stuck between the two seats, and I can't get her out. "Alex! I need you."

He groans but doesn't move.

I unlock Brianne's door and open it, reach across her to shake Alex. "C'mon, we gotta go! The car's on fire!"

Alex wakes up, undoes Brianne's seatbelt, and helps me get her out of the car. I go into the backseat, shocked by how much the car caved-in. Tiffany is wedged in tight and not moving, her face pale. There's no sign of Jackie, the window gone.

My eyes sting from the smoke, but the double vision's cleared. Alex sets Brianne behind a glass-covered bus stop bench a dozen yards away. I walk around the back of the Ford Expedition and spot Jackie on the street, face down, not moving, her head misshapen.

The flames from the Mustang burst into the rear compartment where Tiffany is lying. I'm afraid it's going to blow.

*****

Retrieve Tiffany before Geo. Turn to page 56.

Retrieve Geo before Tiffany. Turn to page 69.

Tiffany's probably already dead, and she looks so squished. No way I'm getting her out on my own. I sprint for the front seat, the plastic melting from the heat. I slap Geo's cheek and yell his name, pray I'm making the right decision. "Wake up!"

His eyes open, but he looks right through me.

"Hold on to me." I reach around Geo's back, helping him out from between the seats and onto the street.

"What happened?" he mumbles as we hurry to the bus stop.

I set Geo down beside Alex, who's sitting up with Brianne's head on his lap. "Be right back."

"Wait," he says. "What's going on?"

"No time," I say, taking off for the Expedition.

The fire flares, and the Mustang's tank explodes, knocking me on my ass.

The Expedition and Mustang are a ball of bright fire, but I can't look away.

"Where's Jackie and Tiff?" Geo asks.

I wish the brightness could blind me so I won't have to face him.

Geo's staring right at me. "Jake. Where are they?"

Alex nods down the road. "Jackie," he says.

"Tiffany?"

I say, "I'm sorry."

Geo gets on all fours and crawls next to me, sees the blaze. "Was she in there?"

The word won't come out, so I simply nod.

He shoves my shoulder and knocks me onto the grass. "What the hell? You let her burn?"

"She was already dead," Alex says. "I seen her."

Again, I just nod.

Geo stands and walks toward the burning cars.

I grab his wrist. "Hold up. We gotta go."

He jerks out of my grasp. "We can't just leave her."

"I'm sorry."

"Those things are everywhere," Alex says. "We got to jet."

Brianne's awake but still dazed.

I ask her, "Can you walk?"

"I think so."

"Okay," I say, trying to gather my thoughts. "We need a car."

Alex and Brianne get to their feet. Geo's walking over to Jackie.

"Help me with her!"

I follow him. "She's gone, man."

"She just moved," he says.

We're about five feet from Jackie when she pushes herself off the street with a scream of pain that cuts through the drugs, my wrecked hearing, and a concussion.

I grab Geo's shoulder. "Don't touch her!"

Blood pouring from her road-rashed face, Jackie crawls toward us screaming like she's on fire. "Help! It burns. It burns so bad!"

Geo tries shaking me off, but I don't let go. "Stop, Geo! She's infected."

"What burns?" Geo asks. "You're not on fire!"

"My brain. My head," she says, crawling closer, blood leaking out of her eyes, nose, and mouth. "It burns so bad! Please, help me!"

I pull Geo back. "She's one of *them*."

Geo takes the step back with me but keeps talking to her. "What can we do to help you?"

Jackie doesn't answer, just pulls herself along the ground.

"Shoot her!" Geo says.

I pull the .357 revolver and aim at her head, but I can't squeeze the trigger.

Geo takes the gun from me and draws down on her. "Don't come any closer! We can't help you! Do. Not. Come. Closer!"

Jackie goes silent, then looks right at me, a deep growl in her throat. She pushes off the ground and lunges.

Blam!

The bullet punches through her head and drops her to the ground. Geo's saying something, but I can't make it out, my ears ringing so loud.

Geo yells in my face. "We gotta get the hell out of here, right now. This place is falling apart!"

"We need a car! Your dad said something about a bunker! Let's just get back to the house!"

Geo reloads the revolver and points to the abandoned cars. "Maybe one of them has keys."

The only car running is the cop car that crashed into us. I run around the burning wreckage to the other side, and Geo follows. The Crown Vic's steel cage on the front bumper is mangled, but the engine compartment seems fine.

There's a dead police officer with his head slumped onto the steering wheel. A deflated airbag's covering his lap. The door's locked, so Geo takes out the revolver and busts the window, kicks it in. He strips down to a sleeveless undershirt and wraps his button-up around his forearm so he doesn't slice himself reaching through the window to unlock the door.

We pull the cop from the car and lay him on the street. Geo grabs the officer's service weapon and two back-up magazines.

"Here," he says, handing over the Glock 17—a full size 9mm with two seventeen-round magazines.

I remove the magazine in it and clear the gun to test if it's loaded. It is. I reload it for a total of eighteen rounds and slide it into the holster Geo just passed to me. Tucking it into my waistband, I feel a little safer, but not much.

"Hey, what the hell are you doing?" someone behind us shouts when Geo unclips the officer's radio.

I spin around and see a bicycle cop about thirty feet away.

The cop drops his bike and draws his pistol. "Get on the ground! Step away from the officer!"

Geo jumps into the car and slams the door shut.

"Stop!" the cops shouts. He's focused on Geo, who's ducked below the window.

*****

Aim for his leg to escape. Turn to page 77.

Aim center mass and put down the threat. Turn to page 106.

This is insane. There's no way Peter's going to be able to hold on to her while she's freaking out. They're past the point of no return, and there's no way I can help them up there.

"Let me go!" Noel shrieks in Peter's face. "I'm going back!"

Both her shoes fall and fly past us, clacking off the concrete several floors below.

Peter keeps calm. "Close your eyes and listen to me."

Noel shakes her head and slides her hand out of the sheet rope, reaching for a higher grip. She pulls herself above Peter, causing him to let go with one hand and grab her by the ankle.

"Stop!" he yells.

Noel keeps going, jerking her ankle free of his grip, sending the entangled sheets swinging out of control. Her feet find the wall, and she scrambles up one, two, three steps, when her right foot slips and she drops hard, her grip on the rope broken.

She plummets past Peter with a piercing shriek.

I reach my arms out to catch her, slamming myself into the bar on the edge of the platform, missing by inches. Her hair passes right through my fingers.

"Fuck!" This shit can't be real. It can't.

Noel smacks the pavement. There's no way she survived that landing.

Everyone goes silent for a second.

"Noel!" Peter shouts from above. "Noel! No! What the hell? No!"

"Get down here, Peter!" Alex yells. "We have to see if we can help her!"

Peter ignores Alex, his cries becoming hysterical. He kicks off the wall, sending himself swinging sideways.

"Stop, Peter!" Alex yells.

The girls are screaming so loud, but nothing's stopping Peter. He swings all the way to the right, as if to aim, and sways back the other way, releasing his grip and crying his fiancée's name. He flies headfirst, landing right beside her.

The thud is nauseating, my body going completely numb. The girls are sobbing, while Alex and Geo rush to the bodies.

The rungs of the ladder are slick with moisture from the humidity. I take each step carefully, praying to wake up from this nightmare before I reach the alley.

Alex and Geo check for pulses and try to get a response.

"Are they okay?" I ask, realizing what a stupid question it is.

Geo shakes his head, staring at the floor. He won't look up.

Alex wipes his tears with the back of his hand. "We've got to get them to help! Quick!"

The thought of carrying their lifeless bodies makes me sick. I don't say anything about how pointless it would be, that they're beyond help. "We've got to get the car first."

Geo nods. "Me and Jake will get the car and come back for everyone. You gotta stay here and protect the girls!" He turns to Alex. "What do your keys look like?"

"It's just a single Escalade key with a Miami Dolphins keychain."

"Don't leave this spot unless you have to." Geo points down the alley at the main street with all the honking cars and screaming people running past. "And don't go that way."

I whisper to Geo, "That's where the parking lot is."

Geo starts in that direction and tells Tiffany we'll be right back. To me, he says, "I told *him* not to go that way. That's *our* job."

Everything is horns, screams, and yelling. My heart and head are pounding. *Oh shit, oh shit, oh shit* is all I can think. We're about halfway to the corner when Geo stops, handing me the holstered revolver along with a handful of bullets.

"You're more useful with this than me. I'll get the keys. You just watch my six."

I don't say a word as I run a quick check on the gun. It's a Smith & Wesson six-shot, .357 Magnum revolver with a three-inch barrel. The bullets are Hornady .357 +P rounds. This thing's going to have some powerful recoil. I tuck the holster in my waistband but keep the gun in hand, my finger on the trigger guard. My thumb is on the hammer, ready to cock it back.

We hurry and hide behind the dumpster about twenty yards off the street. The chaos is all around us, cars gridlocked, horns blaring. Our side of the road isn't moving because of several wrecked cars whose owners are nowhere around.

"Stay low along the building. Use the bushes for cover," Geo says.

I follow his lead, the bushes tearing at my shirt, the gun barely making me feel safer.

"There it is!" Geo points out the valet station beside the resort's main doors. People are still panicking and rushing out of them.

We're almost there when I spot a paramedic on the sidewalk, administering CPR to a man on his back. "Geo! Look!"

Geo bursts out of the bushes toward the paramedic. "Sir! We need your help!" he shouts, running toward the men. "Our friends are badly hurt!"

I follow Geo. When we get within ten feet, the paramedic turns around, exposing the chewed-up skin and blood oozing from his mouth. He howls at us as if he's in excruciating pain.

"Shoot this motherfucker," Geo says out of the side of his mouth as we backpedal.

I snap out of the shock and cock the hammer on the revolver, raising the sights to line up with the rabid man's forehead. He lunges off his victim and sprints toward us. I place one shot between his eyes dropping him instantly, his face sliding across the pavement. The sound of a gunshot creates even more alarmed screams and screeching car tires.

Geo grabs ahold of my shirt and drags me over to the valet station. There are no employees in sight. The kiosk lies on its side, keys scattered all over.

"What do we do now?" I'm frantic, thoughts are racing as I scan the mass of keys, several of them with Dolphin keychains.

"Shit!" Geo says, kicking the kiosk. "I could try to hotwire the car if I knew where they parked it. Dad showed me how using a screwdriver."

"I don't have a screwdriver, and that could take a long time. If you even remember how to do it!" I continue watching the crowds, making sure no more rabid people are near us.

Geo looks around, weighing his options. "If we can't hotwire a car, then we're going to have to steal one."

There are dozens of abandoned cars in the streets, and the valet parking lot is nowhere in sight. Our options all suck.

*****

Steal an abandoned car in the street. Turn to page 57.

Find the key and the Escalade. Turn to page 45.

Car jack someone. Turn to page 132.

I wish there was another way, but Geo can't drive pinned down, and this cop's so amped he'll plug the first one of us who moves.

The officer is only twenty feet away and coming closer, all his attention on the cop car. "Out now or I will fire!" he shouts.

I draw my Glock with lightning speed and fire, the bullet striking his left quad and sending him to the ground, shrieking. I run around the car and jump in the passenger seat, yelling at Geo, "Go, go!"

Gunfire erupts outside. Bullets punch through the windshield, clang off metal, and fly past our heads.

The bullets stop, and Geo throws the car in reverse, switches it back into drive, and swerves around the burnt wreckage, where Alex is crouched with Brianne. They dive into the backseat and bullets fly, blowing out the back windshield.

Geo hits the gas and speeds south on US1, leaving the officer behind. "Turn it up," he says, tossing me the police radio.

"Where are the others?" Brianne asks.

Alex shushes her. "Close your eyes."

There's a burst of noise on the radio. *"Officer down!"* a man says. *"Suspects heading southbound on US1 from One-Sixty-Third Street in a stolen Miami PD cruiser!"*

"Shit," Geo says. "Shoulda taken him out."

"I'm hit in the leg and need an ambulance," the officer says. *"Suspects are armed and dangerous!"*

There's no response on the radio.

"Dispatch? Dispatch, come in!"

"It's just like 911," I say. "They're too busy."

"Oh my God! Ahhh!" the officer screams. *"Help! I'm being attacked! Ahh! Ahhhh!"*

The officer's screams are overpowered by bloodcurdling shrieks. The radio goes silent.

Geo turns right down a backroad. "This will lead us past I-95."

"Why are we in a cop car?" Brianne asks. "Where's everyone else?"

Alex hands her the vape and tells her to hit it. "We were in a wreck. You smacked your head."

"It's the goddamn apocalypse," Geo says.

He's not exaggerating. There are people running through the streets, screaming, cars weaving in and out of the wrecked vehicles.

I grip the Glock and hold it on my lap, keeping an eye on people fleeing houses. Far up ahead is the tall, long embankment holding I-95. I nod at it. "It's going to be nuts on there."

Half a block up, we spot a swarm of flashing blue lights heading our way. Geo takes the next left, right, and left. "That thing still on?" he asks, nodding at the radio.

"Yeah, but radio traffic's gone silent," I say, checking the side mirror to see if the cops are following us.

Geo takes us right, but the street is worse than the others— full of speed bumps and cars blocking our path every several feet.

A teenage girl runs out of the blue house to our left, a purse clutched to her chest. She's heading straight toward us and shouting for help. "Officer! Please, help!"

There's a large man chasing her, and it looks like Geo's going to drive right past.

The girl keeps running for our car, something not right about her hand inside her purse. "Keep going," I tell Geo. "Can't save everyone."

"No, we can't," he says, giving the car more gas.

The girl stops running and pulls a gun from her purse, aims it at us. "Assholes!" she yells, firing, the bullets flying wide.

I don't bother trying to shoot back—she's no longer a threat, and we might need the bullets.

"Jesus Christ," Alex says. "It's a nightmare."

"Everyone, keep your eyes peeled." Geo turns onto the next street so we're headed back to I-95. "Consider everyone else the enemy."

The car is silent, except for the sirens and shouting floating through Geo's busted window. We turn onto the main road. The blue police lights are gone, but a major traffic jam clogs the underpass. Cars are trying to get on, off, and under the interstate in every direction.

"What should we do?" I ask Geo.

"Shit, I don't know."

A flash of blue out my window—might be a hallucination—reminds me we're in a cop car. "What if we throw on the sirens?"

"It can't hurt," he says. "You see a switch for them?"

It's too dark in the car, so I reach for my phone, only to realize I must've lost it in the crash. "I can't see anything."

Geo pulls to the right side of the road and takes out his phone, swiping away dozens of missed calls and texts from Uncle Shawn to get to his phone light. He flips on the sirens and lights, which gets a gasp from Brianne, who's hiding her face against Alex's shoulder.

"Let's do this." Geo pulls back onto the road. As we get closer to the giant traffic jam surrounding the overpass, the cars in our lane move to the side. We're halfway under the overpass when we crawl to a stop. The cars stuck in the narrow tunnel are unable to separate enough to let us through.

"Now what?" Alex says. "We walk?"

With the lights and sirens still going, Geo lays on the horn.

"That's not helping," I say. "They can't move."

Geo cuts the siren but stays on his horn. "Move it assholes," he shouts out the broken window.

The woman in the blue BMW in front of us sticks her middle finger at us.

"Screw this," Geo says, pressing against the left side of her bumper and pushing the car out of our lane.

The BMW's brake lights flash off, and her car smacks the rear of the Ford truck beside her.

An overweight man, with a Miami Dolphin's trucker cap and a Florida Gators T-shirt too small to cover his belly, pops out of the truck. He reaches into the cab and pulls out a shotgun, his face full of hate. The man racks the shotgun and aims it at the woman in the BMW.

The woman's screaming with her hands up, pointing behind her. The guy takes the gun off her and heads toward us.

Geo pulls his revolver but won't have a clear shot through the windshield. I pop out the door and spin to the man, who's now close enough to do damage.

I shout, "Drop it!"

The guy swivels to me and fires, but I fall below the engine, the buckshot blowing by overhead. With a steady stance on one knee, I raise up just enough to fire two rounds into his chest, dropping him.

Everyone is screaming and running from the shooting, leaving their cars behind. I jump onto the hood of the cruiser and wave for the cars in front of us to get to the side, like I'm Moses parting the Red Sea of brake lights.

The BMW punches it, pushing the Ford until we've got enough room to pass. The cars in front of her scoot to the side as much as possible, leaving us a little lane.

I get off the hood and lead the way, when sirens close in from behind. Two Miami Sheriff's cars are flying toward us, screeching to a halt at the beginning of the overpass. Three deputies jump out and line up behind their cars, rifles pointed at our cruiser.

A loudspeaker crackles. "Exit the patrol vehicle now!" a deputy says. "Exit with your hands behind your head!"

There's no way of knowing if any of them are aiming at me or if all their focus is on Geo, but I'm pretty sure they're going to shoot, no matter what. I hope for the best and dive in front of the abandoned van to my right, telling Geo to gun it.

Geo blasts past me, the side of the cruiser scraping paint, squeezing through the cars. The cops open fire, bullets zipping by, slamming into the back of the cruiser.

The small concrete wall separating the lanes is beside me. I jump over it and run, crouched, over to flank the cops from their right. Peeking over the wall, I see most of the officers concealed, except one's leg sticking out to the side of his vehicle. It's about a thirty-yard shot, but they're still firing, leaving me no choice.

I squeeze the trigger, once, twice, three times, the final shot hitting its mark. The cop screams in pain, and his partners fire blindly in my direction.

They haven't seen me, so I duck below the wall and run as fast as I can for the sounds of Geo smashing his way through the traffic.

I make it to the end of the overpass just as Geo pushes the last car out of the way, his bumper dragging underneath him. One of the officers continues to fire his rifle at the cruiser but isn't even coming close.

Geo sees me, whips the car to the left, and lays off the gas just long enough for me to jump in, all four of us staying slouched beneath the headrests. A bullet blows through the back window and windshield. Geo punches it, peeking through the wheel.

No one says a word for the first thirty seconds, the bumper clanking beneath us so goddamn loud. Finally, it breaks off, and we pick up speed.

"Holy crap," Alex says from the back. "Everyone okay?"

"It's got to be a dream." I switch out magazines, no idea how many bullets I've used, everything a blur. "This can't be real."

"Shit never been realer, homie," Geo says. "You still got your phone, Alex?"

Alex says he's on it and leads us southwest down the back roads to keep us out of sight. We pass a sign that says: "Welcome to Hialeah."

"Keep your eyes open for a different car," he says.

Geo humphs. "Maybe the next town."

I've seen enough memes to know Hialeah's a rough place. My spare magazine isn't reassuring. We've only got six rounds left.

"Check it." Geo nods at the large fire burning a few blocks up. He turns left. "Screw that noise."

All the streets on our right have fires on them. We're coming up to the seventh street, which is cast in darkness for the next few blocks.

"This one's clear," I say.

Geo turns right, keeping it to a crawl thanks to all the speed bumps and our car barely holding together. There's no one out, but a few of the houses on my side have doors wide open.

About a hundred yards ahead, dozens of silhouettes mill under working streetlights. I ask, "Should we?"

"Next two streets to the left are cul-de-sacs," Alex says.

"To the right is going backwards," Geo replies.

The gun is keeping me brave. "Just go."

We're about fifty yards away when I spot torches, shovels, and boards being held.

"Let's go back," Brianne pleads.

Alex shushes her, and Geo stays focused.

All the houses on both sides have been broken into, a couple with fires burning inside. The mob of looters is standing in front of a roadblock of large tree branches and trash cans. The two yards to the left and right are only blocked with people.

"They're not friendly," I whisper to Geo, tracking the two men approaching Geo's door.

"Your call," he says. "We go through, around, or back."

*****

Reverse out of here and find another way.
Turn to page 18.

Blast through the middle of the roadblock and shoot anyone that comes near. Turn to page 85.

Swerve onto the sidewalk and drive around them.
Turn to page 14.

We're exhausted, wounded, and never going to escape this hell hole on our own. "We've got to try," I tell Alex. "The Army can save us."

"Screw it," Alex says, needing Geo's help to get up.

With houses burning on both sides, I figure it's safest to stay in the middle of the street away from surprises. "We need something white to wave."

Geo waves his hands above his head at the Humvee headed our way.

Gunfire pops off. A rioter leveling his pistol on the hood of the red sedan we just passed on the left. He's firing at the Humvee, but Geo's already on it, wasting the dude with a quick burst.

The Humvee's .50-caliber opens fire, a hail of bullets blowing right through us. Geo drops like a sack with a bullet to his head, and I stumble back, feeling like I just took three heavy punches to the chest.

I fall onto my back. The warm blood splutters out the wounds, and the night goes dark as the fires burn.

***

Try again. Turn to page 110.

The car is so jacked up I doubt we'll escape the mob, and with our luck we'll break down trying to jump the curb. "Go through these fuckers!"

"Hold on," Geo says, hitting the gas and aiming for the middle of the roadblock.

The mob parts, throwing stones and swinging shovels as we speed at them. We blow the trashcans out of the way and run over the tree branches, but we hadn't expected the goddamn sedan parked right behind it.

There's no chance of swerving, and it's too late for the brakes. The crash booms like thunder, my right collarbone snapping in the jarring halt.

The roar of the mob is almost as loud as the crash. Alex and Brianne scream for help as they're dragged out the busted back window.

I dropped the gun when we hit, and Geo's slumped over, a river of blood running down his face. By the time I get my seatbelt undone, two guys with shovels hop on the cruiser's crumpled hood. The guy in front of Geo kicks the shattered windshield, and the second bashes it in with his blade.

I reach down, hoping to find the gun, but don't. The blade of the shovel slams down, slicing through my shoulder. I scream and the rioter rips the weapon back, my blood spraying my face and the dashboard.

I press back into the seat, but I'm still too close. He switches his grip like he's about to dig dirt and smiles. "Later, homie," he says, shoving the blade at my throat.

***

Try again. Turn to page 83.

These guys are going to catch us any second or put a bullet in our backs. "Go!" I yell at Geo and Alex.

They keep running for the brick wall separating the properties, and I drop to a knee, take aim at the two closest guys that jumped the fence. With only five shots, I can't waste any.

Blam! The one in all black falls face first. *Blam!* His partner spins like a top and drops.

I glance over my shoulder just as Geo hoists Alex over the wall. The group running down the driveway is nearly to me, one of them leveling some kind of machine gun in my direction.

I put a bullet in his head and one into the guy in the bandanna that goes for his gun. Bullets blow past me, one striking my thigh. I block the pain and put down the gunman but have nothing left to defend myself with.

"You motherfucker!" the closest one yells, his board swinging for my head.

I block the blow with my forearm, but it still knocks me to the ground. Geo's calling my name, but he can't help me now. Too many of them surround me, kicking me, jabbing me with sticks.

"Let me at him," a young voice says.

The assault stops, the mob making a circle around me. A boy about ten years old steps forward, a steak knife in his hand, fury in his eyes.

I can't move. My body bleeding from so many wounds, and I can only see out of one eye.

Two guys grab my wrists, another two my legs, spreading me like a starfish.

The boy kicks me in the nuts and I nearly puke, not able to stop his weight from crushing my stomach when he drops on me and straddles my stomach. He brandishes his knife. "You killed my daddy."

"I... I didn't mean..."

"Now I kill you," he says, burying the knife in my chest, tearing it out, and sticking me again and again.

***

The correct choice was to follow Alex and Geo over the fence.
Turn to page 123.

If we just wait for these guys to find us, we're going to get blasted. Our only shot is to surprise them when they enter the bedroom.

I move in front of the closet door and stand, picturing the room's layout. The bedroom door is to my right, the bed to the left, a bathroom on the other side of it.

Geo's whispering something, but I can't make it out through my muffled ears.

There's a loud boom, and the bedroom door slams off the wall. The light flashes on, a bright line shining under the closet door.

"Check the bed," the deep voice says.

"They got guns," the other Haitian with the scratchy voice says. "Careful."

The room goes silent, except for the footsteps. It's now or never.

I kick open the closet door and dive onto the bed, rolling off the far side. Bullets spray overhead and punch holes into the wall.

Crawling into the bathroom, I line up my pistol's front sight straight out the door in case they rush in.

Rounds blast through the bathroom wall, showering me with plaster. Ringing and the vibrations of voices are all I can hear.

Instinct says the guy's out of ammo. I stay low, exiting the bathroom on one knee. A large man with dreads sticking out the side of his hoodie slams a magazine into his AK-47. He spots me as I squeeze the trigger, the bullet piercing his forehead.

The other guy in a hoodie and bandana leaps across the bed and knocks me down, gets fully mounted. He has one hand on my Glock, the other crushing my throat.

I knee him in his balls, which takes pressure off my neck. "Geo!"

The man pulls a four-inch steak knife from his back pocket. He stabs at my face, but I buck him forward, the knife scraping across the floorboard. The guy's off balance, so I take him to the side, trap his leg for the sweep, and end up mounted on his waist.

He tries to stab my ribs, but I pin down his hand, his other still fighting for the Glock.

Geo bursts from the closet and is running for us when the Glock goes off, the bullet grazing Geo's shoulder.

The gunshot scares me, and I lose the knife, looking down just in time to see it sink deep in my quad. I roll off him, screaming, the pain mind-numbing.

The guy scoops up the Glock. His finger's on the trigger, barrel aimed at my chest.

Geo shoots him twice with the revolver, his brains and blood splattering the nightstand.

Holy hell. I've never been stabbed and am not prepared for the pain. A brilliant fire burns through my thigh, blood spluttering around the blade.

"Alex, I need you to help with Jake," Geo says. "Bring a bunch of clothes with you."

Alex comes out of the closet and drops an armload of shirts and pants on the bed. He sees my leg. "Oh shit."

"I'm not feeling so good," I say, a little worried I'm already lightheaded.

"Help me get him on the bed," Geo tells Alex. "Jake, do not move your leg."

The two of them get under me and hoist me onto the mattress, the tiny movement causing a new wave of pain. Geo runs out of the room, saying he'll be right back.

Looking at the blood makes things worse. There's a clump of brain matter on the nightstand clock, which just turned to two.

Alex sees where I'm looking. "The worst afterhours ever," he says, shaking his head.

Geo comes back with a pair of scissors and cuts up three of the shirts.

I ask, "What are you doing?"

"Need a tourniquet." Geo spins each of the pieces into a tight rope, then ties them together. He wraps it firmly above the impaled knife and cinches it so tight my entire leg goes numb.

"I can't feel anything," I say. "It's turning white."

"That's good. Here." Geo hands me a folded shirt. "Bite down on this."

"Why?"

"We got to pull it."

I look to Alex, but he's a mess, sitting on the edge of the bed, head in his good hand. "Maybe that's not a good idea," I tell Geo.

"I'm gonna grab more towels to contain the bleeding," Geo says. "Alex, don't let this guy move."

*****

Do as Geo says and let him remove the knife.
Turn to page 94.

Pulling out the knife is a bad idea. Don't let them remove it.
Turn to page 92.

"No one make a sound," I whisper, hoping that whoever's stomping around the house is going to move on before they find us.

Alex says okay and Geo nods, the outline of his head barely visible in the closet's darkness.

I can't hear what the guys are saying, but it sounds like they're breaking stuff in every room. Their footsteps get louder.

"Not in here," one of them shouts.

"I saw 'em run in hurr. Got to be one of dez rooms."

"Let's cook these muthafuckers."

"Scoot over," I whisper to Geo. "And don't fire until they open the door. You high, me low."

He moves to the side so we're both directly in front of the door, Alex in the corner with his useless pole.

The bedroom door bangs off the wall, and two sets of footsteps clomp into the room. "Clear the bathroom. I got the bed."

"Nothin."

"Empty," someone says from another room.

Steps approach the closet, my hand sweating, finger on the trigger, breath controlled.

The door flies open. Geo and I open fire into the darkness, the muzzle blast making it so I can't see if we hit anything, no grunts or thuds of anyone taking damage.

The barrel of the AK pops out from the side of the door and opens fire, spraying us with point blank bullets, each thud another nail in our coffins.

***

The correct choice was to leap from the closet and surprise them when they enter the bedroom. Turn to page 88.

I've taken a ton of first aid classes and Dad taught me how to handle a bad cut, but I can't remember a thing about impalement. Pulling out the knife sounds like a terrible idea—more pain and nothing to stop the blood from just pouring out.

"We need to keep moving," I tell Alex.

"Stay down," Alex says, taking a puff from the vape pen. "Hit this."

I wave it off. "The longer we wait, the harder it's going to be getting out of here."

"Geo said don't move."

I sit up, the pain making me want to puke. "I got this."

Geo walks into the room with towels and a glass of water. "What're you doing? You can't get up."

"I gotta," I say, using my hands to swing my legs off the bed. The blade tearing muscle. Oh, I just made shit worse, the pain so bad I almost faint.

Geo puts his hand on my shoulder to stop me from getting up. "We gotta pull it. Trust me."

"The tourniquet's gotta be enough," I tell him. "We need to move."

"It's your call." Geo shakes his head. "But I think it's a bad one."

"They're probably searching for us," I say, my thinking so slow I'm no longer sure leaving the knife is a good idea.

"You take both the pistols," Geo tells Alex. He readies the AK and turns back to me. "And you," he says, grabbing my face so I'm looking him in the eyes. "You don't move until we come back for you."

I nod, afraid to hear how weak I must sound.

"Alright," Geo says. "We'll be back in two minutes. Don't move and don't fall asleep."

My eyes close and a slap on my cheek brings me back.

"Jake?" Geo says. "I need you to stay awake."

"Got it."

They leave the room, their voices becoming whispers. My pant leg is completely drenched with blood, a giant puddle pooling on the yellow blanket.

Time ticks by, maybe seconds, maybe minutes, everything silent.

Blam! Blam! Blam!

The rat-a-tat-tat of the AK starts and stops almost immediately.

Alex screams Geo's name.

Blam! Blam! Blam!

I'm wide awake now but so weak.

"Told you those bitches were in here!" a high-pitched voice shouts.

"Two down. One white boy to go."

Footsteps in the kitchen. Headed my way.

I'm as good as dead sitting here, and my only weapon is buried in my thigh. I grab a towel and bite down, pull out the knife, the blood sputtering like a goddamn sprinkler.

"I got down here," someone says.

I put all the weight on my good leg, my left completely useless. Using my hand on the wall, I scoot forward but fall flat, my face banging off the floor, a sharp burst of pain tearing through my stomach.

"Ha! Monster, come look at this stuck pig!"

"Finish this sorry shit."

Blam!

***

The correct choice was to do as Geo says and let him remove the knife. Turn to page 94.

The only thing that's kept me alive this long is trusting in Geo. If he says to take out the knife, that's what we've got to do.

"Alex, let me hit your pen," I say.

He pulls out the pen and hits it first, wipes the tip before passing it over. Like I'm worried about germs.

I take three big hits and can barely control my coughing.

Geo comes back in carrying several white towels and a glass of water. "Drink up," he says, handing me the glass.

The water's cold and tastes so sweet. It's gone in two gulps.

"All right," Geo says. "Lie down and bite hard."

I rest my head on the pillow, sinking my teeth into the folded shirt.

"We're going on three," Geo says.

I grunt.

"One," he says, gripping the handle. "Two." He rips out the knife, blood spurting out before he covers it with the towel.

The agony is unbearable, and I'm screaming through the shirt. Geo's applying firm pressure to the wound, which doesn't help the pain.

"Stay with us," he tells me, but my vision's fading.

**

The clock says 2:19. The fire in my leg reminds me what happened.

Geo walks in and dumps some bandaging supplies on the bed. "Enjoy the beauty rest?"

"I've never hurt like this," I say.

Alex groans from the corner of the bed. "Tell me about it."

"You two need to stop being little girls." Geo makes his best Uncle Shawn impression. "Rub some dirt on it and quit your bitching."

Laughing helps, but not much.

Geo puts together a makeshift bandage out of the cloths and gauze. "Go ahead and remove the tourniquet," he tells me.

The blood flows back to the leg, everything pins and needles. I adjust the bandage and say, "Seems to be holding back the bleeding."

"For now." Geo takes the AK from the dead man's hands. He releases the magazine and checks it before reloading. "Thirty rounds. Here, Alex." He hands him the revolver. "It's only got four shots left. Only shoot if you absolutely have to."

Alex sets it on the bed so he can pick the Glock off the floor. He hands it to me. "How many you have left?"

"Seven."

"Think you can walk?" Geo asks.

"One way to find out."

They ease me off the bed, letting me test out the leg. I limp and it hurts like a motherfucker, but I can move.

We make our way to the front of the house. Alex checks the kitchen, while Geo peeks out the living room blinds.

"The street's quiet." Geo points out an old, empty Ford Ranger sitting in the front yard. The windows have been smashed in, but other than that, the truck looks to be in good shape.

"We'll need keys," I say.

"Nah. Found this." He shows me a small multi-tool. "I'll hotwire it."

Alex joins us. "Driveway and backyard look clear."

"We're taking the truck out front." Geo heads for the hallway. "Follow me."

We enter the bedroom closest to the truck. Geo opens the window and removes the screen. He slides out, Alex right behind him. They both help me down so I don't put too much weight on my leg.

"Stay here," Geo tells us, pointing behind the flower bed with the tall bushes.

Walking with the AK in hand, Geo approaches the Ranger. He reaches in through the already-smashed windshield and pops the door open. His phone lights up the cab as he searches around the steering wheel. From the tone of his grunts, it sounds like he's having trouble.

They're hard to hear, but I make out voices. Down the street, several people in hoodies and bandanas are sprinting for the far intersection, where more people are gathered.

Geo sees them and dives into the tailgate. Alex whispers that we should join him, and we hurry over to the truck. There's no room in the tailgate, so Alex and I crawl under.

The mob at the corner must be at least forty people thick. Part of the mob runs to a house across the street and sets it on fire.

Alex and I both have our firearms pointed at the crowd. "Don't fire unless we have to," I warn him.

From the alley to our left, more masked rioters appear. "Burn it! Burn it all," they scream, setting fire to the house we were just in.

No one's seen us, but they're only fifteen feet away. There's nothing stopping them from torching the truck, but the only place we can go is the group of tall bushes close to the street, about the same distance.

*****

Scramble into the bushes. Turn to page 107.

Stay under the truck until the rioters pass. Turn to page 97.

The night nearly looks like day with the houses burning on both sides of the street, illuminating dozens of rioters carrying torches and weapons. There are way too many of them to risk moving out from under the truck, especially with my leg wound. "Stay put," I whisper to Alex. "Only shoot if you got to."

He nods, turns his attention to the other side of the street. "I got over here."

"Check." I scoot so I can cover this side.

"Holy shit," Alex whispers. "Here they come."

I calm my breathing and keep my eyes open for those with firearms, counting at least five handguns and a submachine gun. No telling what else is in the vicinity.

The night is so loud with all the chants, the screams, the shots. This is hell.

"Hey!" Someone shouts from behind me. "Under the-"

Blam!

My head smacks the chassis as Geo's AK goes off above.

Everyone on my side turns toward our truck, but I don't wait to see what they're going to do. I put a bullet through the guy with the submachine gun first, and empty the Glock on the rest of them, hitting about half my shots as they dive for cover, the brave sprinting for us.

A glass bottle breaks a few feet in front of me, burning gasoline igniting my shirt and skin. Alex isn't moving behind me, nowhere for me to go except into the fire. I drop the Glock to cover my face and roll through the flames.

"Get 'em!" someone shouts as I try to get to my feet, my hair on fire, my leg unable to support me.

Something heavy slams into my side, a blast of pain from my broken ribs.

I fall on my chest and try to army crawl, but the fire's burning my head and my left arm can't pull me forward.

Geo tumbles out of the Ranger's bed, smashing face first on the concrete a few feet away.

"Where you going, Smokie?" someone asks with a grunt.

Something slams into my upper back, piercing me in several places, metal smashing into my spine and ribcage.

Whatever's stuck in me rips out and I can't stop screaming. I roll onto my back, the blood pooling all around me. The thug in a black hoodie raises his garden rake and brings it down, all five prongs burying in my stomach.

He rips out the rake and they laugh as blood spurts from the holes.

***

The correct choice was to scramble into the bushes.

Turn to page 107.

This guy looks like a trapped racoon, ready to lash out. I'm afraid saying something will make him shoot, but it's our only chance.

"Sir, we just want to get home." I keep my gaze off to the side so he won't worry about me reporting him. "We didn't see anything."

"Nope, nothing," Geo agrees.

The girls swear the same.

"Please," Jackie says, half-hidden behind me. "We didn't do anything."

The man aims the gun at my face and keeps it there. "Anyone moves and you're first." With his back to the wall, he slides to the side. "I just want to get to the stairs."

"We're not moving," I assure him, praying Geo and the others understand that's an order. "Please, go."

He keeps sliding along the wall until he's past us. The man spins around and bolts for the stairwell, slamming the door shut behind him.

Holy shit. I let out a sigh and lower my arms. Jackie and I are both shaking violently.

JD is curled on the floor with a thousand-yard stare, his mouth hanging open. The white letters spelling "Security" on his black shirt are stained dark red.

Alex and Peter argue about which way to go.

"Damn," Geo says, "that dude wasted him." He gets between me and the bouncer's body. "What do you think, Jake? How are we gonna get down?"

"The stairs have got to be even worse now." Brianne sits on the carpet to rub her swollen ankle. "I say we wait a couple of minutes and figure this out."

Pop! Pop! Pop! More gunshots erupt from the stairwell. More screams.

Everyone jumps.

"We're not going that way!" Peter says. "The elevator's also not an option!"

Geo points at the open door the shooter came from. "Safety first. Let's figure this shit out in private."

Alex and Peter help Brianne inside the apartment while Geo and I usher in the others. Geo locks the deadbolt behind us.

Clothes are littered all over the floor, dresser drawers hanging open. The apartment looks ransacked, but there's photos on the wall of the man who shot our guide. In these pictures of him with old women and babies, he doesn't exactly look like someone capable of killing.

Alex and Peter take Brianne into the bedroom and put her on the bed.

"Get me ice," she says through her tears.

Peter runs toward the kitchen. Alex sits beside Brianne and strokes her arm.

"Call 911!" Brianne shouts.

Tiffany's on the loveseat with Jackie, both bawling, and I'm standing here, frozen.

"What the hell?" Alex says from the bedroom. "It's busy."

Peter jogs past me with a plastic bag full of ice. "What is?"

"911." Alex holds up his phone to show us the screen. "It's never busy."

Peter tosses Brianne the ice and pulls out his own phone to call. After a few seconds, he says, "Dude, this is *not* good."

Geo digs through all the drawers in the kitchen, then rummages through the closet.

I pinch myself to make sure this isn't a drug-induced dream. "What are you looking for?" I ask. "We need to figure out what to do."

Geo moves to the nightstand drawers. From the bottom one, he pulls out a holstered revolver. He slides out a Smith & Wesson .357 magnum. "Ta da."

"Nice job," I say as he pulls out a box of bullets from the drawer, loading six into the revolver.

Geo dumps the rest of the bullets in his front left pocket and re-holsters the gun, sliding it into his waistband. "Hope we won't need it, but holy shit."

Alex turns on the TV and finds a news channel. A reporter is standing on the side of the highway, where a row of police cars block all four southbound lanes. Cars pack the northbound freeway bumper to bumper, leaving Miami.

"As you can see," he says, pointing at the row of cars being directed off the highway, *"authorities are closing off all major entry points to the city and urging everyone to evacuate immediately."*

Honking cars and the blare of sirens make it hard to hear him, but there's no mistaking the look of fear etched on his face.

"I repeat, do not attempt to enter Miami-Dade County. We have dozens of reports of attacks by large groups of rabid people across the city. If you cannot evacuate, get to a safe place and lock yourself in until rescue arrives."

I nudge Geo's shoulder. "Your dad was right."

Geo doesn't say anything. Alex turns the TV louder.

"The National Guard is being brought in, and aid from the Coast Guard is also being enlisted," the reporter says. *"According to eyewitness reports and cellphone videos, the rabid people attack victims with their bare hands and bite them. Unable to determine the cause of this behavior, the federal government has advised everyone to evacuate Miami-Dade County immediately. Miami-Dade will be locked down until further notice."*

"What in the hell are they talking about?" Peter asks, sounding panicked. "They can't be serious!"

The newsfeed pans back into the studio, where a graying anchorman is sitting in shock. *"Thank you, Jason. You stay safe out there. We hope everyone in the Miami-Dade area has a safe and speedy evacuation."* He clears his throat. *"Breaking video coming through. We have been warned that this video is graphic and viewer discretion is advised."*

The scene jumps to what appears to be security camera footage from a gas station. A dark Chevy SUV pulls up to the pump closest to the front door. A balding, middle-aged man slides out of the driver's door and pulls his wallet from his pocket. He inserts his credit card into the pump, completely unaware of the woman sprinting toward him at full speed. The gas pump flies out of his hand, and he hits the ground harder than a quarterback getting sacked. The attacker straddles the man's waist and claws his face. The man flails his arms and tries to fight back, but the crazed woman tears a chunk of skin from his neck.

"We saw one of those freaks earlier!" Geo shouts. "Jake, we gotta get back to the house!"

Panic is setting in, and the girls won't stop crying. Brianne seems the most composed, despite her swollen ankle.

"We've got six floors to get down," Geo says. He taps the revolver's handle. "But at least we've got some muscle."

"So, we leave, right?" Alex says. "My keys are at the valet station."

Geo looks at me. "What do you say?"

The drugs have placed me in a dream-like state. "I'm following you."

"I'll be right back," Alex tells Brianne.

Peter stays with the girls, while I follow Alex and Geo into the living room. They open the window and look out.

"Side of the building," Geo says. "An alley."

"And check it," Alex adds, sounding hopeful. "There's a fire escape about three floors down."

Geo points out a ladder. "That's our out. We can grab some sheets and blankets to make a rope that'll reach it."

"Everyone grab as many sheets as you can find," Alex says. "Strip the bed."

I stick my head out the window, and the humid air makes me nauseous. The steel platform they're talking about looks so small. This doesn't feel like a good idea, but what other choice do we have?

Jackie walks up, puts her hand on my back. "We're not really going out there, are we?"

"I don't think there's another choice. It's either that or risk getting shot in the stairwell."

Her face deflates, and she walks back to Tiffany.

Geo and Alex drop a pile of sheets on the couch and tell me to get started. I grab the two thickest linens and tie them together, pulling as hard as I can to test the knot. When I'm finishing my third knot, they drop off a few more blankets.

Geo takes the end of the makeshift rope and ties it around the large wooden pillar beside the kitchen, a few feet from the window. Alex and Peter gather the girls while I keep tying the sheets, tugging the rope with each new addition.

"Think that's long enough?" Alex asks.

"One way to find out." I toss the entangled pile of sheets and blankets out the window.

The end of the rope slaps the metal fire escape.

"Perfect," he says. "Even got a couple inches of slack."

"So, how do we do this?" Peter asks. "I've never done this shit."

Geo grabs the end of the rope. "Here's how to safely tangle your hand and foot into the rope. If you do it like this, nobody falls."

He wraps the rope around his wrist and ankle in a manner allowing him to control his descent while he holds on. Slowly but surely, he scales his way down floor by floor. In under a minute, Geo plants his feet safely on the fire escape platform.

"Who's next?" Geo hollers.

The girls are visibly shaken and clearly aren't ready for the challenge. Even Peter and Alex seem hesitant. My mouth goes dry, and my palms are sweating. I walk to the window, lacing my hand and foot into the rope as Geo did. Hopefully, they can't tell how scared I am because I'm frantic on the inside, flashing back to all the YouTube fails of extreme parkourists who've fallen to their deaths from buildings.

"Ain't nothing to it but to do it!" Geo hollers.

I nod and slip out over the side of the window. This is it. One mistake and I'm dead. I start down the side of the building, positive that, any second, the sheet's going to give.

The sounds of screams and sirens fill the air, but it can't take my focus off the wall in front of me. My heart rate has to be over 200 beats per minute. I take a deep breath and blow it out, descend one step at a time. Finally, my feet hit the fire escape.

"Okay, who's next?" Geo shouts, taking control and acting like he isn't even phased.

Alex pokes his head out. "Hold that end still. The girls are coming down next. Me and Peter will go last."

Jackie makes her way out of the window, with her foot and hand entangled in the sheet rope. She's in tears, slowly coming down. After what seems like an eternity, her feet are on the fire escape. Through uncontrollable sobbing, Tiffany makes it down smoothly. Brianne is slower, but does a great job with just her one foot. It's Noel's turn, but she is frozen at the window, screaming to go back.

Peter says he'll escort her down last. Alex goes next, easily faster than anyone.

Everyone else goes down the ladder, but I stay on the fire escape to hold the sheet tight one last time for Peter and Noel.

Though I don't like the idea of two people on the sheet, at least Noel is tiny. "Go for it," I yell up to them.

Peter's trying to calm Noel down as she scoots her legs out the window. "Come on, baby," he tells her. "You've got to trust me."

It takes her a minute, but she finally appears, her foot and hand tangled closely to his in the makeshift rope. Peter holds the sheets and Noel simultaneously. They begin their descent, but she's hyperventilating before they even descend one floor.

"I can't," Noel cries. The rope shakes violently with her attempts to climb out of Peter's grasp and back up the rope.

*****

Let Peter handle Noel. Turn to page 73.

Climb the sheets to help Peter bring Noel under control.
Turn to page 40.

I hate to do this, but right now the world is a war zone and everyone but us is the enemy. I can't risk trying to shoot the cop's leg with an unfamiliar gun, no telling if I'll hit him or if he'll be able to return fire.

"Drop the weapon!" the cop says, taking aim at me.

My Glock's already locked in, and I squeeze off three shots, all direct hits.

The officer stumbles back and falls. I run around the car and find the passenger door's locked. "Geo! Open it!"

Blam! Blam! Blam!

Two bullets blow by me, the third smacking me in the right shoulder, my gun falling to the ground.

I drop to a knee to pick up the Glock, turn to the officer who's somehow sitting up, his gun held in both hands, the barrel aimed at my face. "Shit." I hadn't considered he could be wearing a bulletproof vest.

I've only got one option with my right arm useless, and it's a terrible one. I raise the Glock with my left hand, but the cop's gun is already blazing, his bullets ripping right through me.

***

The correct choice was to aim for his leg to escape.

Turn to page 77.

There are too many rioters for us to open fire, and we're dead if they find us under this truck. "We've got to get to those bushes," I whisper to Alex.

"What about Geo?"

"I'll grab him."

The crowd of rioters moves to the next house and sets their torches to the roof. They're focused on the fire, their backs to us.

"Go," Alex says, crawling out the left side.

I slide out to my right and stifle a scream as I get to my feet. Grabbing Geo from the cargo bed, I say, "Come on."

"Hey," someone shouts from behind. "Who the hell is that?"

A rioter in a purple hoodie is pointing his torch at Alex, who's running for the bushes by the street. Alex scrambles out of sight. The rioter pulls his torch back over his shoulder, ready to throw it at the bushes.

I raise the Glock and drop him with one round to his head.

The gunfire gets everyone's attention. The rioters next door run at us with torches. One torch goes flying toward Geo, who's crouched in the truck.

The torch bounces off Geo's shoulder and lands in the Ranger's bed. Geo jumps down and sprints for the bushes. I'm limping right behind him, tearing open my wound and waiting for a bullet to end it all.

Geo parts the way through the bushes and grabs Alex, who's waiting for us on the other side. "Keep going," Geo shouts, pointing across the street.

The rioters open fire, and bullets blow through the bushes. Alex spins like a top, a bullet blowing a hole through his right bicep, his scream piercing my nearly-deaf ears.

Geo pulls us behind the thickest tree. "Run across the street. I'll cover you."

We've got to move, but not like that. "We need our ammo,"
I say, picking up the revolver Alex dropped. "Let me draw their
fire."

Before he can say no, I scramble to the far edge of the
shrubbery. A bullet misses, sending dirt into my eye. No one's in
the open. All the rioters are firing from behind cars and fences,
the burning houses behind them.

I stick my arm out of the bush and empty the revolver in the
direction of the rioters. Gunfire tears apart the bush as I hurry
back to Geo and Alex. "That way," I say, waving them down the
street.

We barely make it to the next house when shots blast past
us and ricochet off the concrete.

Geo turns around and unloads the AK in three-shot bursts
at the flashing enemy barrels.

"Watch it!" Alex says.

Turning to see if he's talking to me, I kick the curb with my
left foot. I stumble onto the sidewalk, but my right leg can't hold
my weight. A ripping pain goes through my thigh. With both
hands holding a weapon, I land on my shoulder.

Geo stops firing. "Get up!"

I want to lie here and die but can't let them get killed
protecting me. While I'm crawling to stand, the rioters stop
shooting. Their gunfire is replaced with their screams and the
shrieks of the bath salt people.

Two houses down, someone runs out of the flaming carport.
The sprinting shadow leaps into the shrubbery and comes out
the other side on top of a rioter who was hiding. With the fires
burning behind them, they're just shadows and their bodies
become one, their shrieking screams sounding straight from
hell.

Alex is waiting for us at the next house. Geo and I catch up
with him, sticking to the middle of the street because the houses

on that side are burning out of control, the flames licking the yards. We hobble up the street, a wounded squad. The only reason we're even moving forward is for the sake of the man next to us.

There's movement up at the next intersection—a crowd of rioters running right for us.

Alex and I peel off to the right and fall onto the grass behind a small brick wall. Geo stands his ground and empties the AK at them.

Instead of the AK fire suppressing the crowd, they fire back. Geo dives beside me, bullets smacking the wall and blowing by overhead. This mob is heavily armed.

"We've got to move," Geo says, taking the revolver from me. "They'll surround us."

The barrage of gunfire stops abruptly.

"Shit, they must be moving," I say. "Going to flank us."

Geo peeks over the wall and ducks back down when more shooting erupts.

Nothing's hitting near us, so I roll to the edge of the wall and look toward the intersection. The rioters are firing down the street to our right.

We're in a war zone, the *rat-a-tat-tat* of a heavy machine gun firing. Rioters drop like flies.

Geo reloads the revolver. "Anything?"

The rioters keep shooting down the street, but they're no match for the hail of bullets. Every one of them is mowed down in under a minute.

A huge, armored vehicle rolls into the intersection with a man on top behind a 50-caliber roof-mounted machine gun.

"It's the Army in a big-ass Humvee," I say.

Geo pops up. "That's our way out. Ain't nothing bringing *that* down."

"Think we should?" Alex asks. "They might think we're bad guys."

*****

Stay hidden behind the wall until the Humvee passes.
Turn to page 113.

Run for the Humvee with hands up.
Turn to page 84.

Take off west and find a car.
Turn to page 111.

The Army has already devastated the neighborhood, and there is nothing to say they won't mow us down too. We're never reaching safety if we don't move. "West," I tell Geo. "Gotta get a car."

He nods. "Follow me. I got point."

Geo stays low and near the bushes, Alex next. I do my best to keep up, watching out for threats from the rear.

Small arms gunfire pops off behind us, but it's someone across the street shooting at the Humvee. The gunner on the Humvee turns the .50-caliber on the guy and neutralizes him.

"Keep moving," I say, hoping they don't see us in the shadows. Up ahead on our left, inhuman shrieks echo. A huge pack of rabid bath salters are storming down the street straight for us.

Geo stops running and readies his gun. "Wait until they're closer."

The Humvee's spotlight shines on the crowd, the .50-caliber mowing them down. Half still crawl forward but no longer pose an immediate threat.

"Jesus Christ," Alex says with a sigh. "Thank God for the Army."

The spotlight leaves us in darkness, and the .50-caliber unleashes in another direction.

The shrieks outlast the gunfire. "Go, go," Geo says.

We don't hesitate, sticking to the front yards of the houses, our guns trained on the mindless bath salters who feed on their dead and wounded, dragging their bodies our way.

Up ahead, both corner houses burn, leaving us nowhere to go but through the dead and wounded bath salters filling the street.

"To the right," Geo says at the intersection. "Stay with me. Only headshots and only if you got to."

This is a terrible idea, but we're out of choices. Geo steps off the sidewalk, weaving in and out of the bodies, staying away from the ones eating and slurping, and stepping over the motionless.

"Holy shit," Alex keeps repeating under his breath, his aim covering our left.

"We got this," I tell him, my focus on our right and rear.

Blam! Blam!

I spin around to Geo with his AK, a shattered bath salter's skull inches from his feet. "Careful," he says. "Fuckers are fast."

Alex swivels toward me, fires two bullets right past my leg, sinking them into a bath salter crawling right for me.

It isn't stopping, so I leap back and put one in its head, forgetting my leg is useless until I'm falling.

"Get up!" Geo screams, shooting over my head, picking off more bath salters crawling for us.

Alex helps me to a knee and fires his last shots at a woman scrambling for us, leaping for my back.

I finish her off and attempt to stand, but she landed on my calf, her hand wrapped around my ankle.

Geo goes full auto, his magazine clicking empty. Alex runs for the sidewalk, but a bath salter trips him up and jumps onto him. Two others join the attack, blood flying.

"Geo," I say, knowing how this ends. "Take it." I hand him my gun. "I'm done."

He sees the hand on me and wipes the filth that has splattered his face. "We both are," he says.

"Do it," I tell him.

He takes the Glock and puts it to my temple. "I love you, brother."

***

Try again. Turn to page 110.

The houses to our right and left burn brightly, and angry rioters rage behind us. Seeing how they tore apart the neighborhood, I don't trust the Army.

"Maybe we go west? Find a car?"

The Humvee is heading our way. I grab Geo's arm so he doesn't get up.

A rioter wearing all black runs behind the red Civic across the street. He levels his pistol on the car's hood and fires at the gunner, every round missing.

The gunner returns fire, shredding the car and dropping the rioter.

The Humvee turns on a massive spotlight, shining it along the front yards and down driveways.

"Keep your heads down," I whisper.

The spotlight reaches our yard and stops on our position. The loudspeaker crackles. "Put your hands behind your head! Do it now, or we will fire on you!"

I leave the Glock on the ground and stand, putting my hands behind my head and all my weight on my left leg. Geo's up and following orders, but Alex can only raise his burnt arm, his face screwed up in pain.

"Hands up or—"

The shrieks of rabid people ramp up. The spotlight turns down the road we just ran from. The gunner aims in that direction and opens fire for five seconds straight.

The spotlight spins back on us, the gunner firing directly over our heads.

We all hit the grass, Alex screaming because he landed on his arm. None of us are hit. The gunner is still firing, but nothing is hitting the wall.

Geo points behind us at the fern-covered fence, the rabid people scaling the fence, running straight for us as the machine gun mows them down. The creatures are bloodthirsty but mortal, some of them continuing to crawl but no longer a threat.

I've only got nine rounds in the Glock, Geo with six. The gunfire ceases.

Geo's right next to me, but I yell, "We've got to go with them. They got to help us."

Geo shakes his head. "I don't..." He shuts his mouth and turns toward the Humvee and the mob of rabid people charging its rear.

Two soldiers exit the vehicle and empty their rifles on full auto, dropping dozens but not making a difference. It's like a flood of flesh—one goes down, two more trample over them, at least a hundred in the pack.

The stampede slams into the soldiers about twenty feet in front of the Humvee. The gunner directs his fire into them, but the soldiers are gone, several of the infected already too close to shoot with the machine gun. They jump on the Humvee, but the gunner keeps shooting, slaughtering the rest of the mob.

A chubby, bald guy in basketball shorts grabs the gunner by the back of his collar and pulls him from the machine gun. A brunette in a pink bra and panties is right behind him, swatting at the gunner's face, his arm holding her back.

A pistol goes off, and the brunette's hands shoot to her face. The gunner fires again, and she falls off the Humvee. The chubby guy pulls the gunner onto the street, where an elderly couple with matching yellow robes waits for the meal.

We're trapped on both sides by burning houses. Behind us is littered with bodies, but the gunner won't be there to save us if there's another wave. I get Geo's attention.

"We gotta go that way," I say, pointing up the street, where rabid people are slamming into the Humvee's windshield, trying to get to the driver.

Gunfire erupts from the opposite side of the intersection. It's a small group of rioters, but they're heavily armed, bullets bouncing off the Humvee and tearing through the rabid mob.

The Humvee shoots forward at full speed, running over everyone in its way. It swerves before hitting the light post, but as it evens out a volley of bullets rips through the passenger side window.

The Humvee takes a sharp turn to the left and is coming at us. There's no way of knowing where it's going to hit.

Geo jumps up and pulls my arm toward the street. "This way!"

*****

Wait for the Humvee to pass. Turn to page 117.

Follow Geo and run into the backyard. Turn to page 9.

We're hitting the bath salters no matter what, but there's still a chance to avoid killing the fleeing family. I grab hold of the wheel and turn it toward me, realizing too late that Geo was already turning that way to take out the attackers.

"No!" Geo screams as we blow through the two women and directly toward the pumps.

My world blows bright white, and we're airborne but only a split second, the ceiling crumpled against the concrete pillar, no seatbelt on to prevent my neck from snapping.

We slam back to the ground, my limbs useless, my thinking slow. I'm facing the driver's side. Alex took the hit harder than me, his skull split and brain visible. Massive flames char him through the shattered windows.

My face is melting but I can't scream, can't move.

***

The correct choice was to let Geo drive and whatever happens happens. Turn to page 62.

I want to run for the backyard, but Alex is curled on the ground behind the brick wall. The Humvee's headed right for us. It's too dangerous to leave. I pull Geo onto the grass, and we hunker down even tighter behind the small wall, hoping the Humvee doesn't hit us.

The Humvee smashes through the bushes to our left and slams into the fern-covered fence. The accelerator's full throttle, but the tires spin up dirt.

Geo grabs the empty AK and sprints over to the Humvee. Alex and I get up and go after Geo, who is cocking the rifle over his shoulder like a baseball bat.

I pull my gun, thinking Geo's about to hit someone, but he slams the rifle into the already-damaged passenger windshield, putting a hole in the glass.

Geo sticks the barrel of the AK into the hole and pries it even wider. He drops the rifle and reaches in through the shattered glass, slicing his forearm to unlock the vehicle.

Alex is watching our backs, so I turn to the intersection where the rioters and rabid people are keeping each other busy.

The accelerator stops and Geo grunts, pulling out the driver who looks our age, a bullet hole in the side of his head. Geo drags the soldier onto the grass and jumps in the front seat.

"Get in!"

I'm throwing open the back door for Alex when a rabid woman in a nightgown rushes up and lunges for him. Before I can think, I put a bullet through the side of her head. Geo grabs Alex and rushes him into the back, slamming the door shut. I climb into the passenger seat and wipe my palm on my pants, regripping the Glock, hoping I don't have to fire it again.

Geo puts the Humvee in reverse and spins us around, speeds toward the chaotic intersection, veering as far right as he can. "Alex, did you get bitten?"

"I don't know, man. I can't feel shit other than my fucking arm."

A ponytailed blond in blue jeans and a halter top leaps for the Humvee, her bloody face disappearing under our hood, her body becoming a speed bump. Other rabid people break off from the battle and bounce off our vehicle. A heavyset Haitian man in a hoodie and blood-rimmed mouth runs face-first into my window.

We're nearly out of the intersection when we're peppered with small arms gunfire. The Humvee's armor holds up, and Geo smashes the accelerator. We leave the carnage behind us, finally heading west.

The next block is empty, except for some solo rabid ramblers feeding on corpses. The next block is even better with fewer people, but Geo's not saying a word, his eyes darting everywhere. We're all just waiting for another attack.

"Holy shit, dude," I say. "This is insane."

We pass a sign indicating we're entering the city of Doral, the streets quiet and calm.

"Anything in the glove box?" Geo asks.

There's nothing but an owner's manual. Nothing on the seat either, but my foot kicks something on the floorboard. It's a SIG Sauer M17, full-size, 9mm handgun. I pull out the extended-box magazine, which has fourteen rounds in it.

"Here," I say, handing the Glock off to Geo. "Got six or seven shots left."

Geo stuffs the Glock in his belt loop and takes out his phone. He dials home and puts it on speaker.

The call picks up before the first ring finishes. "Geo?"

"Dad? Whatsup?"

"I thought you were dead for the last two hours," Uncle Shawn says, surprisingly calm. "Where are ya, son?"

"We're barely five minutes away. Are you in the bunker?"

"I am, but I don't know if we can letcha in. We're gonna have to discuss it," he says, sounding kind of sad.

"What? Who the hell is *we*? Can't let me in! You're shitting me!"

"Is it just you and Jake?"

"Me, Jake, and Alex," Geo says, super pissed. "You've met Alex before!"

"Son, this is not the time to act like a child. And don't worry who *we* is. *We* have to discuss it. I'll call you back."

Geo bangs the steering wheel with his fist. "He hung up on me! What the hell is he thinking? We're not infected!"

A puff of smoke floats from the backseat. I spin, thinking fire, but it's just Alex hitting the vape pen, holding it with his left arm, which looks like a burnt hotdog covered in ketchup and dirt. Sweat's pouring from his forehead, his eyes barely open. His right arm's still bleeding profusely from the wound above his elbow. The bullet must've stopped in the bone because there's no exit wound.

I take off my shirt and turn it into a tourniquet, leaning into the backseat so I can tie it around his arm.

Geo stops bitching about his dad and asks, "How is he?"

"Uh, I mean..."

"How you doing back there, Alex? A-Train still moving, right?"

"I'm... I'm here, man. I'm here," he says, his speech slurred. "Are ya takin me home, now?"

What he needs is a hospital from losing blood and severe dehydration, but I know that's not happening.

"Hey, man, I can't take ya home. That's too far back the other way. But Imma take you to my house, and you'll be safe there, okay?"

"I..." Alex takes a deep breath. "I don't think your dad wants me there, man," he says with his exhale.

"Well, he doesn't have a choice. It's my house too, and you're staying with us! I'm gonna look out for ya!"

Alex lays his head back against the seat and closes his eyes.

We turn onto southwest Eighth Street, the last road before Swisher Road. We're close.

Geo's phone rings. *Uncle Shawn.*

Geo answers it. "We'll be there in less than five minutes! I'm heading straight to the bunker."

"Son, we talked it over," Uncle Shawn says calmly over the speaker. "We're gonna let you and Jake—"

"No shit, you're gonna let us in! Alex is coming in too! Whether you like it or not."

"You and Jake," Uncle Shawn says, keeping it cool. "That's it. I'm sorry for your friend, but he's gonna have to find somewhere else to go. You can leave him in our house, but he can't come here."

"Who the hell is *we*? Who're these people getting to decide who comes into *our* bunker?"

"They're *my* colleagues. And *we* have the final say. Period. Don't bring him... or else."

"Or else *what*?" Geo says. "Screw this! We're turning down Swisher now."

Geo drops his phone on the seat and pounds the steering wheel with his fist. "Can you believe this shit?"

It sucks, but I also know Shawn wouldn't do something like this for no good reason.

"It's going to be all good, Alex," Geo says. "Don't worry."

Alex is slipping in and out of consciousness, doesn't even acknowledge Geo.

We speed down Swisher Road through the darkness, the trees blocking out any moonlight. When we pull into the yard, there is an all-black, Suburban SUV with no license plates sitting in the driveway.

"Should we make camp in the house? You got tons of guns."

Geo lays off the accelerator and looks at his house. "No, Dad said the bunker for a reason."

"Check it out," I say, pointing toward the kitchen window. "There's someone in there."

"Shit, probably just one of Dad's flannel friends rounding stuff up."

*****

Take Alex to the house, with or without Geo. Turn to page 133.

Help Geo take Alex to the bunker. Turn to page 126.

I'm not scared of dying and know I'm really fucking close. That's why I'm going to keep my cool and pretend I don't care what they do with Alex.

I'm running on fumes, my mind a mess, my body so much worse. There's absolutely no way I can carry Alex back to the house. I doubt I can even make it there on my own.

No, we need in that bunker, and there's only one way to change Uncle Shawn's mind. With force.

"Fine. Just give me a sec." I lean over to say goodbye to Alex.

"Get inside," the masked man says.

Alex looks dead, but I pretend he's got hold of my wrist and won't let it go. "Help me!" I say, continuing my struggle to break free.

The man sidesteps to my right, and I make my move, my elbow flying for his face.

He's a pro and swivels out of the way, bullets flying, blowing holes through my chest, dropping me to the dirt.

The gunfire stops and all I can hear is me coughing up blood. The man in the black mask walks up to me, his boots an inch from my face. "Nice try, champ," he says, stepping over me and entering the bunker. The door shuts behind him.

***

Try again. Turn to page 129.

We can't fight the entire mob. I grab Alex to pull him up, my fingers digging into his crispy, cracked skin.

"Oww!" he screams.

I didn't mean to grab his hurt arm, but at least it got him to his feet. "Sorry, man," I say.

He runs past me for the fence Geo's scaling. I help Alex over, and gunshots ring out from behind, a bullet whizzing by and blasting through the board.

Throwing myself over the wall, I chase after Geo and Alex, who are tearing through the backyard. Geo takes us left, then right and left again through the maze of backyards. Alex is falling behind, and my legs are burning, my lungs on fire.

We're running past a brown house's carport when Geo stops and points to the open side door. "Get in," he says, pushing Alex into the house.

A quick check behind shows all clear. I join them inside and lock the door behind us.

"Damn," Geo whispers. "They tore this place *up*."

Even in the dark, it's easy to see the house has been ransacked—furniture tipped over, blood on the walls.

Geo grabs an ironing board and uses it to barricade the door.

I take Alex through the house and lead him into the furthest bedroom. Geo's right behind us and closes the door, turning the cheap lock.

The closet is big enough for all three of us. I slide the door shut and put us in pure darkness, sitting down to Alex's left.

My hearing is coming back. I can't make out what they're saying, but it sounds like the mob's surrounding the house. "What are we going to do?" I whisper to Geo, hoping he can hear me.

Geo flips on the closet light. "Top off your gun," he says, searching the shelf.

Between my two magazines, I only have nine bullets left. I load them all into one magazine and put it back in the Glock.

Alex is in severe pain, the light showing he's not exaggerating. His shirt has melted and become a part of his red and brown skin. It looks like a bacon-wrapped chicken breast in the middle of being cooked.

I grab a blouse dangling above me. "Here, Alex, we should wrap your arm."

He shakes his head. "Don't touch it," he says through clenched teeth.

Geo breaks off the wooden clothes rack and hands it to Alex. "Better weapon than nothing."

"We just stay in here?" I ask Geo.

He shakes his head, takes out his phone, and texts Uncle Shawn that we're still coming.

Alex reaches into his pocket, pulls out his vape pen, and takes a huge rip.

I ask for the pen because what does it even matter? Everyone's dead or dying, and the police are after us. I hit the pen harder than I have all night and cough uncontrollably.

There's a loud crash nearby, like a door getting kicked in. One man, then another, yells something I can't make out.

Geo flips the light off and puts us back in darkness, my throat burning so bad as I stifle the cough.

Banging and stomping comes from the other room. "I think dey in hurr," a deep voice says. "For real, for real, Imma put one of deez rounds in der foreheads when I find 'em."

"I'm telling you, dawg," another voice says, "dey kept running across da street and hit dem otha backyards."

"Nah, fuck dat, man. Dey ain't dat fast. I swear to God, dey ran in hurr. They killt my brotha and my cousins. Imma find em'n barbecue 'em."

The voices go silent, but their footsteps give them away as they move toward the front of the house.

"Check all the closets," the deep voice says.

Doors bang open, and I grip my Glock tightly with both hands. Geo and Alex move to the back of the closet, readying their weapons. I join them, my senses hyper-focused because of the weed.

The footsteps are coming closer.

*****

Wait until they open the closet, if they even open it at all. Turn to page 91.

Leap from the closet and surprise them when they enter the bedroom. Turn to page 88.

Whether it's the swamp or Uncle Shawn's conversation, a big part of me does not want to go with Geo. If I insist, I know he'll go with me to the house, but Geo seems convinced his bunker is the safest place to be. "You got us this far," I tell him. "Whatever you think is best."

"The bunker," he says with a nod, not sounding so sure. Geo drives around the right of the house and follows the strip of grass to its end at the swampy Everglades. He slams the Humvee in park and gets out, opening Alex's door.

I join Geo and help him get Alex out of the vehicle. The sounds of the swamp and distant shrieks and screams send a shiver down my spine.

"How far do we gotta go?" I ask, looking down the dark, thin, man-made trail running along the murky swamp. "He can barely walk."

Geo squats and hoists Alex on his back. "We've got this," he says, putting on his phone's flashlight. "Get out your gun and stay close."

Holding the SIG makes me feel a little safer. "All right, I'm behind you."

Geo's phone lights up several feet in either direction. We trudge along the trail as fast as we can, my wound on fire, Geo breathing heavy.

"We're almost there," he says, pointing at a small light up ahead where the trail widens into a circle of ground risen from the swamp. In its middle is a square cinderblock building about seven feet tall with a steel door on the south side.

Geo sits Alex down against the building. "Help keep him awake," he tells me

I can't kneel with my leg, so I tuck the SIG into my waistband and bend over, reassuring Alex he's going to be okay.

"Where we at?" Alex mumbles, sounding drugged.

Geo bangs over and over on the steel door.

There's nothing but the sound of the swamp and cries of chaos.

Geo stops pounding and calls Uncle Shawn. The phone rings longer than it has all night, no one picking up.

The steel door slowly opens. Geo tries to force it, but it continues at a steady pace, a bright light shining out from the bunker.

A broad-shouldered man wearing a dark flannel shirt, black pants, and black gloves fills the doorway. He aims his submachine gun at Geo's chest. "Step back several feet," the man says behind his white medical face mask. "Do not get near me."

Geo does as he says, hands in the air.

The man exits the bunker and steps to the side, his gun covering all three of us.

Uncle Shawn walks out, mask on, pistol holstered. "Don't hurt him. He's my son," he says calmly. "I told you not to bring him, Geo. Have you touched any of the rabid people?"

Geo puts his hands down and gets in Uncle Shawn's face. "No, Dad! I haven't! And who's this guy? You bring a friend, I bring a friend! Thought you'd at least be happy I'm alive!"

"I am, son. But now's not the time for emotional decision making. This is a crisis."

"Alex's part of the reason I even made it here alive!" Geo is almost in tears. "He stays."

"I'm sorry, son, but he can't."

Another man dressed like the first but with a black mask, exits the bunker brandishing an M4 rifle, a spare magazine in his pocket. He steps to me, shoves his assault rifle in my face. "Remove the gun and set it on the ground."

I do as he says, extra slow so he doesn't fire.

"And who the hell is *this* guy?" Geo yells. "You get two guests, and you're telling me I can't have one who saved my life? Bullshit!"

Geo shoves Uncle Shawn, but the man in the white mask is quick, kicking out Geo's legs, planting him on his back. Before Geo can get up, Uncle Shawn flips him over, pinning him with a knee between his shoulders. The other man gathers Geo's arms and cuffs his hands.

"Which one is your nephew?" the one in the black mask asks, pointing the M4 at me then Alex. "The conscious one?"

Uncle Shawn gets up, shaking his head while Geo keeps cursing. "Roger."

I step in front of Alex because I know what's coming.

"Get out of the way," the masked man orders.

Geo's right. This is bullshit. "No. I'm taking care of him. He's fine with me."

"Move out of the way."

Geo lifts his face from the dirt. "What the hell, Dad? What's he doing to my friend?"

"Son... I told you not to bring him here."

"What? You're gonna kill him? You can't!"

Uncle Shawn nods at Geo and says, "Get him inside."

The man in the white mask picks Geo up and pushes him toward the bunker.

"Just let him leave," Geo begs.

"Yeah," I say. "He can stay with your friends in the house."

Uncle Shawn turns to me. "I don't have anyone at the house."

Geo screams at him to stop, holds on to the doorframe. "Don't do this, Dad!"

Uncle Shawn grabs Geo's free arm and forces him down the stairs.

Alex is all but out of it, his limbs twitching. Shawn's colleague aims the M4 at my face. "Get in the bunker. Last chance."

*****

Accept our fate and enter the bunker.
Turn to page 137.

Refuse and walk Alex back to the house.
Turn to page 130.

Take out the gunman and force our way into the bunker.
Turn to page 122.

He is clearly ready to blast me, but I stare down the barrel, not giving a fuck. "I wouldn't be here if it weren't for Alex," I tell the masked man, not sure if it's true, everything a blur, my mind and body on fire. "I'll get him help."

"Don't be stupid, Jake!" Uncle Shawn yells from the bunker.

He tilts his head to the side and re-aims the rifle. "Move, kid."

"Fucking shoot me! I'm taking him!"

His finger tenses on the trigger.

"Leave them," Uncle Shawn shouts. "Lock the door."

The man dismisses me with a nod. "Good luck," he says, entering the bunker, the door swinging shut behind him.

The lights cut out, the night so dark I can barely make out Alex slumped against the wall. "Come on, man," I tell him. "We've got to go. There'll be a med kit at the house."

I don't know if I can walk all that way, even on my own. Carrying Alex isn't an option. "Alex," I say, my voice blocking out the distant shouts and shrieks. I give his shoulder a shove. "You gotta wake up. I'm sick, man. I can't do it."

He grumbles, shifts against the wall.

I search the ground for a thick branch I can use as a walking stick. There's a low growl when I pick it up, but I can't tell where it came from.

I limp back to Alex. "This is it," I tell him. "Last time. I swear."

He's awake, making some kind of noise, but he's not getting up.

I slap Alex's cheek, and his eyes snap open, a crazed animal about to attack. I jump back, but my leg gives out and my back hits the dirt. I scramble for my gun, but Alex is already on top of me with a burst of energy he hasn't shown since we escaped the club.

Spit falls on my face as Alex snaps at me, my forearm against his throat. I try to fight, to get my other arm free, but it's pinned and I'm so weak.

Alex claws at my eyes, blinding my right one. I scream and cover my face, but he's already sinking his teeth into my neck, growling as he tears out a chunk.

***

Try again. Turn to page 129.

It'll take way too long to find Alex's key, if it's even still here, and there's no telling if we'd be able to find the Escalade or get it out of the parking lot. I turn to the street, figuring the abandoned cars were left for good reason, no expectations drivers left the keys in them. "We gotta jack one," I tell Geo. "But don't hurt anyone."

He takes off for the street. "You're the one with the gun!"

Shit. I chase after him, all my senses on high alert, watching out for the police, rabid bastards, and panicked people.

The street is a mess with trucks pushing abandoned cars out of their way and jumping over curbs. Geo points out a silver SUV with an old lady looking petrified behind the wheel. "There!" he shouts. "Her!"

I run to the front of the car, staying on the sidewalk where she can see me and the gun, while Geo fails to open her door.

He bangs on the window. "Open up!"

She shakes her head and keeps her eyes straight ahead.

"Open up! We'll help you!" Geo says, which I hope is the truth.

"Forget it, Geo! We gotta find-"

I spin to my right and see the van barreling down the street. No time for us to move. The van jumps the curb and smashes into Geo, the grill blasting my hip. My head bangs off the windshield and my body flies, crashing onto the sidewalk.

Everything blazes white hot pain, my legs shattered. A bone sticks through my jeans. I'm facing the building and Geo, whose head is cracked open, dripping all over the dirt.

I pull myself up, blood streaming down my face. I wipe it away with the back of my hand as I turn toward the roar of an engine and the Mustang flying right at me.

***

Try again. Turn to page 76.

"Uncle Shawn isn't known for changing his mind, and I'm not abandoning anyone," I say, nodding toward Alex.

"I'll make him," Geo says.

"Yeah, maybe, but I'd rather take my chances inside your house. Just drop us off. You can check out the bunker on your own."

Geo slows to a stop. "You sure?"

"Sure as I can be."

"Alright," he says, driving us to the garage. "Guns and ammo first."

Geo and I get out of the Humvee, the not so distant shrieks and screams reminding me we're nowhere near safe.

Geo opens the back door. "Come on, Alex."

Alex is a mess, barely able to stand on his own. "Where we at?" he asks.

"My place, homie," Geo tells him. "Gonna get you fixed up."

I ask Geo if the people inside might be a problem.

"If they are, they won't be for long," he says, motioning to his AK. "Punch in the code."

I punch in the eight digits and the steel door rolls up.

We step into the garage and sit Alex down at the table with my range bag on it. I set down my SIG and grab my trusted Glock, load it while Geo switches his AK for the shotgun.

"What're you guys doing?" Alex asks, his speech slurred, eyes barely open. I hope that it's his blood splattered across the left side of his face.

"Making sure it's all safe," Geo says, skirting the ATVs and heading for the door leading into the house. "I'll be back with supplies to get you all healed up."

"Yeah," I say, nodding for Geo to open the door, my gun aimed over his shoulder so I can eliminate any threats.

Geo opens the door. The hallway clear, we pass Geo's bedroom on the left, Shawn's on the right.

Someone's banging around in the kitchen, but there are no voices, only grunts.

Geo swivels around the corner. "Oh fuck!" he shouts. *Boom ! Boom!*

A body falls at Geo's feet, half its head missing. But a second person leaps out and slams into Geo's chest, the shotgun clattering on the tile.

The rabid bastard wraps his arms around Geo, biting at his face.

My first shot grazes the man's head, drawing his attention. The second punches through his forehead and drops him.

Geo's hysterical, screaming about his face. He holds his hand to the ragged hole in his cheek, blood streaming down.

"Shit, shit, shit," I say, not sure how close I should get.

A door flies open behind me and bangs off the wall. A husky old lady in a pink nightgown runs right for me, blood smeared all over her face.

My shot catches her shoulder, but she's not stopping. She barrels into me, and I can't brace myself with my bad leg. We collapse together, all two hundred or so pounds of her on top of me.

I bring up the pistol, but she clamps down on my wrist, her teeth tearing skin. I punch the bitch in the face, but she isn't letting go, whipping her head back and forth.

Geo grabs hold of her hair and rips her head back, but she's not releasing my wrist. I grab the gun with my left just as her hair tears free and she dives for my neck.

Her teeth sink into my throat, but I've already got the barrel to my temple, my finger squeezing the trigger.

***

The correct choice was to help Geo take Alex to the bunker.

Turn to page 126.

There are too many guys to fight, and we've got to get the hell out of here before the exits get too crowded. "Let's go!" I shout at Geo, but he and Alex are already fighting.

Jackie pulls me back and points at Brianne and Tiffany who are running for the main exit. Ahead of them, men and women are getting knocked down and trampled. "Come on!" she screams in full panic mode.

I hate bailing on Geo and Alex, but someone has to protect the girls.

"Go! Go!" I yell, taking the lead with Jackie's hand around my wrist.

Tiffany and Brianne hit the cluster of bodies blocking the exit. We're still about twenty feet from the door and I can't see any way we're making it through. "We've got to go a different way."

Tiffany pounds on the back of the guy in front of her and eats his elbow when he spins around. Brianne gets two handfuls of his hair and yanks, calling him an asshole.

I go to pull the girls away but get slammed into them, my head snapping back from the force.

Jackie's screaming my name, squished between her friends and the mass of people behind us.

It's getting hard to breathe and my right arm is trapped. I push with all my strength to open some space in front of me, freeing my hand. When I look back to Jackie, she's dropped to her knees. I bend down to pick her up, and someone scrambles over my back. My legs buckle.

Everything is dark down here. The walls press together. Knees knock into my head and back as more people climb over me.

I suck in a deep breath and try to stand, but there's no chance. The weight of the crowd forces my body flat to the ground.

A sharp pain rips through my cheek and teeth are knocked loose by someone's stiletto, blood filling my mouth as all hope is lost.

***

Try again. Turn to page 38.

I feel like the world's biggest traitor, but I have no choice. Plus, Alex is Geo's friend, and Uncle Shawn already made the call. All I can do is say, "Sorry," and limp into the bunker.

There's electrical equipment and containers filling the small room, along with the flight of stairs I can't get down on my own.

Geo is struggling at the bottom of the stairs. Uncle Shawn yells, "Sit your ass down and shut your goddamn mouth or he's going to sedate you."

Alex grunts as the man in the black mask drags him away from the building.

"Jake! Get down here," Uncle Shawn demands.

I can't take my eyes off the doorway. In an instant, Alex leaps off the ground at the man dragging him.

"Oh shit!" The masked man leaps back and opens fire. Alex's body goes limp.

Geo screams, "No!!!!!" A struggle ensues followed by silence.

I feel sick and can't think. Everything is so fucked up.

Uncle Shawn hurries up the stairs and instructs me to wrap my arm over his shoulder, to let him bear my weight. "You've lost a lot of blood."

I'm so lightheaded I'm afraid I'm going to collapse, and we're only two stairs down.

Uncle Shawn drops me into the steel chair next to Geo, who is nodded off, drooling, hands cuffed to his. "Don't worry, he's just sedated."

To my surprise, Uncle Shawn drops a pair of handcuffs and a bottle of water in my lap. He backsteps across the room and sits directly across from me, his pistol aimed at my chest. "Cuff your right hand to the chair."

I stutter. "Why?"

"We don't know if you've been compromised. Your friend was infected."

I can barely think, struggling to piece together the timeline of this nightmare. Did I get infected? I cuff my right arm tightly to the chair. "I don't know. I don't know if I got infected. I don't think so. I hope not."

"I hope so, too."

"Good," Uncle Shawn says when the cuffs click closed. "And Jake..."

I look up, too afraid to speak, not sure what noises I might make, whether I'm still fully me.

Uncle Shawn keeps the pistol in hand, resting it on his lap, the barrel facing me. "No matter what, Jake, I want you to remember your father would be proud of you. Always was. Try to just relax and let's see what happens over the next few hours."

Relax? That thought alone makes me want to laugh, but I keep my mouth shut. I don't feel infected, but all I can think of is the throbbing pain in my leg. Let's hope I'm still here in the morning.

The End

For more fun-filled deaths, please check out the sequel *TNTD: Back at Grandma's House* and the rest of the

Try Not to Die series.

Available on Amazon

Out Now:

At Grandma's House
In Brightside
In the Pandemic
In the Wizard's Tower
Wild West
At Ghostland
At Dethfest
Back at Grandma's House
On Slashtag
In a Dark Fairy Tale
At the Meadow Spire Mall
The Shadowlands
In This Damned House
In Arcranium
Escaping the Cult
Super High

In the Works:

In Brownsville
In the UK
By Your Own Hand
In Area 51
In the Tournament of Mortem
In Hollow 2
In a Prison Riot
At Desperation House
In a Video Game
Between the Worlds
In 25 Perfect Days
Hanging with the Homies
On Werewolf Island
With a TBI
With many more soon to be announced

Download Your Free Copy

Includes the first two chapters and one or two death scenes
from each of the first 14 books in the *Try Not to Die* series.

How Did You Do?

We hope you enjoyed the book and wouldn't mind giving us a little feedback. Thank you so much for your support.

Scan below to answer a few questions about your reading experience.

Try Not to Die Merchandise

For the latest Try Not to Die hoodies, shirts, puzzles, blankets, and signed copies, visit Mark's store:

ABOUT THE AUTHORS

Steve Montgomery

Born and raised in Florence, SC, Steve Montgomery's journey in martial arts began at a small country gym, where he first crossed paths with author Mark Tullius. Their friendship continued over the years, eventually bringing them together again in South Florida when Mark interviewed Steve for *Unlocking the Cage*.

Steve is the head of the American Top Team Striking Program, where he leads boxing, kickboxing, and MMA training. As a fighter, he maintained a perfect 6-0 amateur MMA record before going pro, earning a 10-6 record against world-class opponents. A Bellator veteran, *The Ultimate Fighter 25* contestant, and two-time UFC competitor, Steve has spent over 15 years training—11 of them at Top Team Headquarters in Coconut Creek.

Beyond his own fighting career, Steve is a Brazilian Jiu-Jitsu black belt under Bob DeLuca, with ranks earned from legends like Rafael Rebello and Ricardo Liborio. He has also made a name for himself as a highly respected coach, cornering fighters in UFC, Bellator, *The Ultimate Fighter*, *The Contender Series*, ONE FC, Titan FC, and countless other professional and amateur events.

Now, Steve brings his experience and passion for storytelling to the page, blending his deep knowledge of combat sports with gripping narratives that keep readers hooked.

Mark Tullius

My writing covers a wide range, with fiction being my favorite to create, twenty or so titles under my belt. There are 16 titles in my interactive *Try Not to Die* series and 24 more in the works. I also have two nonfiction titles, both inspired by a reckless lifestyle, playing Ivy League football, and battering my brain as an unsuccessful MMA fighter and boxer. *Unlocking the Cage* is the largest sociological study of MMA fighters to date and *TBI or CTE* aims to spread awareness and hope to others that suffer with traumatic brain injury symptoms.

I live in sunny California with my wife, two kids, five cats, and one demon. Derek the Demon pops in whenever he's bored and makes special appearances on my social media.

You can also get your first set of free stories by signing up to my newsletter. This letter is only for the brave, or at least those brave enough to deal with bad dad jokes, a crude sense of humor, and loads and loads of unhappy endings. Derek and I would love to have you join us!

Scan below to Visit Mark's Website

Horror

90 Short Stories

Out Now from Vincere Press

Listen to the Books

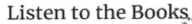

You can listen to several books in the Try Not to Die series, short horror stories , suspense novels, or nonfiction. Find your next listen at your favorite retailer or www.MarkTullius.com

Nonfiction

MMA

Exploring the
Motivations of Fighters
100 gyms
23 states
400 interviews

Brain Health

Facing fears of
dementia from
repetitive blows to
the head.

Jiu Jitsu

Current Project
A coffee table book
featuring Mark and
his family training
around the world.

Connect with Try Not to Die

The TNTD series has its own social

media pages.

Check them out on IG at

https://geni.us/TryNotToDieOnIG

In addition to Instagram,

you can also check them

out on TikTok at

https://geni.us/TryNotToDieOnTikTok

To watch Derek the Demon, book reviews,

podcast clips and more.

https://geni.us/TulliusYouTube

CONNECT ONLINE

Connect with Mark

Mark enjoys sharing his
passions on social media.
Check him out on IG at
https://geni.us/TulliusIG

In addition to Instagram,
you can also check him out on
Tik Tok at
https://geni.us/TulliusTikTok

To watch Derek the Demon, book reviews,
podcast clips and more.
https://geni.us/TulliusYouTube

Made in United States
Orlando, FL
20 July 2025

63112842R00085